COUNTING DOWN WITH THEODORE BROWN

COUNTING DOWN WITH THEODORE BROWN

DANIEL DEVENNEY

ALLEN&UNWIN
AUCKLAND • SYDNEY • MELBOURNE • LONDON

First published in 2026

Allen & Unwin Aotearoa New Zealand
Level 2, 10 College Hill, Freemans Bay
Auckland 1011, New Zealand
+64 (9) 377 3800
auckland@allenandunwin.com
www.allenandunwin.co.nz

83 Alexander Street
Crows Nest NSW 2065, Australia
+61 (2) 8425 0100

Our authorised representative in the EU for product safety is Easy Access System Europe, Mustamäe tee 50, 10621 Tallinn, Estonia, gpsr.requests@easproject.com

A catalogue record for this book is available from the National Library of New Zealand.

ISBN 978 1 99114 235 1

Cover design by Alissa Dinallo
Cover illustration by Sophie Watson
Text design by Carla Sy
Set in Plantin MT Pro 11pt
Printed and bound in Australia by the Opus Group

10 9 8 7 6 5 4 3 2 1

FSC www.fsc.org MIX Paper | Supporting responsible forestry FSC® C001695

For the wallflowers, I see you

CONTENTS

CHAPTER ONE

ONE — AIMEE MANN

My name is Theodore Brown. If I had friends, they'd probably call me Theo.

I'm not entirely sure why I'm writing this. My therapist thinks putting my thoughts on paper will help with my communication skills, and at this point I'll try anything. But if this turns into some cliché teen drama, I will rip it to pieces and burn it myself.

I don't get teen tropes, even if I do happen to be a teenager. I turned 19 today, which means I only have another 365 days of this insufferable purgatory to go. Woohoo! I'm one step closer to adulthood and still have no fucking idea what I'm doing.

Not that there's much *to do* in this Podunk town. I regretfully reside in a small town in Indiana. It's called Fairview, which is ironic, considering there ain't a thing fair about it. It's one of those places in between much cooler places. People stop long enough to top up on gas, maybe grab a bite to eat if they're desperate. Then they hightail out of here, leaving nothing but dust and crickets in their wake.

That's why I'm spending my birthday on this newfound journey to enlightenment through writing. That was sarcasm. I hope that's obvious by now. But I figure today is as good a day as any. New beginnings and all that jazz. Like I said, I've reached a point where I'll try anything. Otherwise, I'm destined to spend the rest of my life alone. And as much as I try to convince the world that I'm okay with that, nothing terrifies me more.

I've spent most of my 19 years on this planet with my head buried in a book. Reading has always been my drug of choice. Whenever reality lets me down, I find a new world to explore. Why stay here when I can slay vampires, or become a wizard, or travel through time and space? When it comes to escapism, nothing beats a good story.

But it's time I faced the truth and wrote my own. Hopefully, writing this hot mess down will help me understand what the hell is going on. Who knows, maybe someone out there will relate? I mean, there's gotta be others like me out there somewhere.

There's also a second motive behind this little experiment: I'm studying creative writing at Fairview Community College. I finished my first year a few days ago. I asked my professor if there was anything I could do to improve my writing over summer break, and the jackass told me to ditch the library card. Can you believe that guy? What kind of English professor discourages reading? He said if I want to be a great writer, I need *real-life* experience. When I politely asked him if he could be less vague, he told me to go out and party with friends, travel, fall in love and get my heart broken . . . That's professor-speak for *Get a life!*

So, that's my goal this summer. I'm going to get a life. Thereby pleasing my therapist and English professor in one tragic attempt at becoming less socially inept — ergo, a better writer. The trouble is, parties and dating are so far out of my comfort zone, they're in a different hemisphere.

I see my therapist once a week because I have trouble connecting with people. Like, at all. I don't even make eye contact with my own mother. This tends to make people uncomfortable. Apparently, it's awkward holding a conversation with someone who won't look at you. So, most of the time nobody talks to me. Honestly, I don't blame them. My behaviour is a little odd. But in my defence, I have a valid excuse. And that's where my story gets weird.

My problems connecting with people are not because I'm shy or insecure or I wasn't given a puppy named Sparky as a child. If only it was that simple. I avoid looking directly at other people because when I look into their eyes I don't see what everybody else seems to see. At least, not entirely. Sure, I see two pearly white eyeballs in the middle of each face. But the irises and pupils are always missing. For me, they're replaced with a number. Black swirls spread out like ink to form this number, and everyone I meet has one.

I shit you not — this is my unfortunate truth. It's been this way for as long as I can remember. I know how eyes are supposed to look because I see them in photos and on TV. It's only in real life they go all *Twilight Zone* on me.

It wasn't until I started school that I knew I was different. That's when the trouble began. Ms Bradbury taught our class to count and unwittingly changed the trajectory of my life. She gave names to these squiggly shapes I saw in people's eyes. And this gave them power.

I remember vividly the first time I started to identify those shapes. I was six. It was a typical Saturday morning at the Brown residence. Dad and I were eating breakfast on the living-room couch so we could watch cartoons. Saturday mornings were reserved for two things: Lucky

Charms and *SpongeBob SquarePants*. This was our sacred tradition, and under no circumstances could it be broken.

Dad looked like a different person on weekends. He reverted to a scruffy teenager when he didn't have to go to work. He ditched the shirt and tie and spent most of the day in his *Star Wars* dressing gown. He was like a big curly-haired kid. I felt more like his best friend than his son on days like those.

After breakfast, we'd play air guitar to one of his records. That morning I chose 'A Night at the Opera' by Queen. It was one of our favourites. I lost count of how many times we rocked out to 'Bohemian Rhapsody': I was the Brian May to his Freddie Mercury. Dad really went for it and I thought he was a rock star.

We collapsed on the floor after yet another epic performance. I hopped onto his belly, and we gasped for air between giggles. Eventually I caught my breath, looked him dead in the eyes and began to sing.

'One-five-nine,' I chirped loudly and out of tune.

'That's not right, Silly Billy,' Dad said. 'Start again and count to 10.'

I waved my index finger in his face. 'I'm not counting, Daddy. I'm reading.'

He cocked his head and squinted. 'Reading what, buddy?'

'Your eyes,' I said in the most matter-of-fact tone my six-year-old self could muster. 'One-five-nine,' I repeated.

He was obviously confused. So was Mom when he told her that evening. But she wasn't overly concerned and said it was probably just a game. After all, I'd been learning to count, and after school I'd plant myself in front of the TV and watch colourful puppets sing about math. Mom assured Dad it was a harmless phase.

Sadly, she couldn't have been more wrong.

One hundred and fifty-nine days after that carefree morning, our lives were irrefutably changed. That was the day I learned the ramifications of the mysterious number that occupied my father's eyes. I watched the number shrink with each day that followed. It counted down like a doomsday clock until there was nothing left in each of his eyes but a tiny zero. The morning my dad zeroed out, he kissed me on the cheek before he left for work as he always did. I never saw him again.

He was hit by a car and killed instantly.

At least that's what the doctor told Mom. I suppose they always tell you it was instant. I mean, it's not like a doctor is gonna say, 'He suffered tremendously for hours before passing.' I try not to think about that part.

I blamed myself for a long time, replaying that morning over and over. Wishing I'd warned him. Wishing I'd done everything I could to stop him. I'd known in my gut something was wrong. Those tiny black zeros sent chills down my spine. But I was just a kid. Even if I'd thrown an epic tantrum, it wouldn't have made a difference. Dad had to work. He couldn't afford to stay home just because I threw a wobbler.

He worked at the local post office. It's only a couple blocks from our house. Mom used to joke around and say things like, 'Don't get lost on the way, honey.' I found this hilarious. My dad was Superman. He couldn't get lost. And he certainly couldn't get hurt. He was invincible. Or so I thought, until I learned even heroes die.

Ever since that day, nothing has scared me more than the number zero. I convinced myself that once it appeared in someone's eyes, their time was up. The numbers are a little more complicated than this, but that's a tale for another day. It's my birthday, after all. And I have the sudden urge to hug my mom.

Best thing about a hug — no eye contact necessary.

CHAPTER TWO

SUNGLASSES AT NIGHT — COREY HART

Plot twist — my birthday wasn't a total suck-fest. I even got a sick new pair of shades. I don't usually pay much attention to how I look. I'm mostly a jeans and T-shirt kinda guy. But there are two things I've gotta have: sunglasses and Dad's old leather jacket.

Mom gave me the jacket last year when I turned 18. I was reluctant to try it on at first, afraid my skinny ass would drown in it. But I'd been ogling it in Mom's closet for years. It still smells like Dad and it's just like the one James Dean wears in the black-and-white poster on my bedroom wall. James is on a motorcycle and smoking a cigarette, looking like a total badass. You know the one. It's iconic!

That's another thing I had in common with Dad. We used to watch all the classic movies starring actors like Gene Kelly, Rock Hudson, Marlon Brando and, of course, my personal favourite James Dean. I'd stare in wonder as Dad mimicked all the actors' lines. He was great at impressions. He said those old movies reminded him of his dad. I never met my grandpa. He died young too. But I feel like I know him because Dad talked about him so much.

Even now, most of the actors and musicians I love are dead. That probably sounds morbid. But James Dean was *the man*, and not in that archaic male-archetype sort of way. He was masculine and sensitive. Tough and artistic. He taught me that I could be more than one thing while also giving a firm middle finger to toxic masculinity.

Mom buys me sunglasses every year for my birthday. This year she truly outdid herself. She found vintage Ray-Ban Wayfarers at our local thrift store and got them for an absolute steal. Those bad boys go for a small fortune online. They're the same ones Corey Hart wears in the 'Sunglasses at Night' music video. I'm *never* taking them off!

These bring me to a total of 13 pairs. I'll admit, it's a little excessive. But everyone has their vice. I saw a news story about a woman who owned a second house for storing her colossal shoe collection. In comparison, I'm Joe Moderation.

Hold up — I should probably provide some context for this unusual family tradition. There's method to our madness, I swear.

The sunglasses thing started when I was seven. It was my first birthday without Dad. Mom took me to the mall and said I could have anything I wanted. She insisted we deserved at least one day of reckless spending. Whether or not we could afford it was another story. She was in her *overcompensating* phase.

Most seven-year-old boys would've taken their mom to the cleaners. But she knew I wasn't that kind of kid before she made the offer. I think part of her wished I was. A spoiled kid would have been considerably easier to deal with. But the only thing I wanted was my dad back.

Special Occasions are the hardest days after you've lost someone, and those first few were the worst. Dad tended to go overboard on things like birthdays and anniversaries, but he'd even throw a mini celebration every Friday just to welcome the weekend. The man could make laundry day fun. He believed a positive attitude and a good sense of humour were the two most important things in life. Back then, we didn't need to spend a lot of money to have a good time.

'You gotta grab the good times with both hands and milk 'em for every drop, kid,' he'd say. I don't know if he stole the line from an old film star, or if it was something he made up. But I loved the bravado in his voice when he delivered it.

Mom and I had it easy then. We just sat back and enjoyed the ride. But now that he was gone, one of us had to take the wheel. The trouble was, neither of us knew how.

'Come on, kiddo,' Mom said after an hour of aimlessly roaming the mall. 'There must be something you want?'

'Can we go home and watch *Singin' in the Rain*?'

I don't do well in crowds, and that old movie was like a security blanket. It still gives me the warm fuzzies when life gets too intense.

'Sure, sweetie, as long as you promise to help me eat all that birthday cake.'

'I promise.'

'Okay, let me pick up my contacts before we go.'

Mom started wearing contact lenses shortly after Dad died. Without him around, she was constantly losing her glasses. He'd always reminded her where she'd left them. He'd grab them from café tables, bus stops and shop counters. As soon as Mom started scrambling and ransacking her handbag, he'd present them with a cheesy grin.

'Where did I leave them this time?' she'd ask, relieved and frustrated simultaneously.

Dad was never a dick about it. My parents had each other's backs. That's just how they were.

I checked out the sunglasses while Mom collected her prescription. I was minding my own business, trying on a comically oversized pair, when an elderly woman appeared in my mirror.

'Don't they look spiffy on you,' she said.

I whipped around and froze. I must've stared at her for a good two minutes. She had blueish hair and wore a brightly coloured tracksuit paired with thick purple sunglasses. I vaguely recall her asking if I was okay. But I was too dumbstruck to respond. I just stood there slack-jawed. Eventually, she clutched her fanny pack and marched off. She shook her head and muttered something about young people having no manners anymore. But I wasn't trying to be impolite. My mind had just been blown.

Her sunglasses hid her number!

How had I not realised this before? I could lead a normal life. All I had to do was get everyone in the world to wear sunglasses. Every second. Of every day. For the rest of my life.

Okay, so it wasn't much of a cure. But it was something. It was the first spark of hope I'd had in a long time. I ran to Mom and insisted we both buy a pair.

Luckily, it was summer, so it wasn't the oddest request. She was startled by this sudden burst of enthusiasm, but mostly she seemed relieved I was excited about something.

We put on our new shades as we left the opticians, and I immediately changed my mind about going home. Now that I wasn't constantly worried about catching a glimpse of Mom's number, I had a new lease on life. Suddenly, the mall was brimming with possibilities.

We went to all the places we used to go with Dad . . . We had ice cream at a '50s-themed diner, played mini golf and even went to the record store. This was a big deal! We hadn't used the record player since Dad died. It was his baby, and dust had been the only thing to grace its platter since. Mom bought Lana Del Rey's *Born to Die* album and said we could listen to it when we got home. I was thrilled by the prospect of music finally returning to our lives.

But when we got home, Mom removed her sunglasses without warning. I recoiled in horror, shrieking as though I'd just witnessed a grisly murder. She rushed to my side as I cowered in the corner, covering my eyes with my hands.

'Theodore, what's wrong?'

'Put them back on!' I pleaded.

She gently stroked my cheek. 'Honey, it's getting dark,

and we're inside. We don't need sunglasses anymore.'

I yanked my head away so fast I felt her flinch. 'It's more fun with them on,' I wailed.

'We can wear them again tomorrow,' she said calmly. 'We can still have fun without them.'

She didn't get it. How could she?

'We haven't even cut your birthday cake yet. Go upstairs and get into your pyjamas. I'll get the record player ready.'

I wiped my snotty face on my sleeve and ran upstairs. She didn't say it but she was disappointed. I'd ruined our perfect day.

We came to a compromise when I returned in my SpongeBob pyjamas; she didn't have to wear her shades as long as I could still wear mine. We listened to Lana Del Rey, ate cake and watched *Singin' in the Rain*, and our wacky family tradition was born.

Mom has bought me a new pair of shades every birthday since. They rarely leave my face. I fall asleep in them most nights. I probably look like a pretentious jerk. But I don't care. I'm pretty sure a few people at school think I'm visually impaired, which isn't completely inaccurate, I guess.

So, there you have it: sunglasses . . . One small step for mankind, one huge leap for Theodore Brown!

DISCOVERING 3D GLASSES AT the movies was another small triumph over my affliction. When everyone's got their glasses on, I blend right in. That said, I managed to stand out by going to a 3D movie with Mom for my birthday this year. Now I do realise that going to the movies with your mother is nightmare-inducing to most guys my age. But who invented the stupid rule that you've gotta hate your parents when you're a teenager anyway? It's so lame. I'm not some Norman Bates-type creeper. But it's just me and her now, and we look out for each other. That's way more important to me than looking cool.

I noticed a few guys from college sniggering at us during the movie. But I didn't care. It's not like I have a reputation to uphold on campus. I'm mostly invisible. Not even the wallflowers notice me. I'm like the brick wall underneath the wallpaper. People know I exist but I'm easy to ignore.

Mom rarely has company either. She went on the odd date a couple of years back, but they always seemed to end before they'd begun. Lately, it seems like she's given up.

Most of my parents' friends were mutual. After Dad passed, most of them slowly drifted away. Dad had always hosted barbecues, birthday parties and game nights. He was a real social butterfly. He'd flutter from one end of the room to the other, making sure everyone had a drink in their hand and a smile on their face. I guess it was too painful for everyone to get together after he died.

Mom tried inviting people over. But it wasn't the same. It only seemed to make Dad's absence more prominent. It was like there was this huge black hole in the centre of the room, sucking everything inside it like some malicious, fun-draining vortex. That's not exactly conducive to a party atmosphere.

There was one friend who used to come over a lot. Her name was Gilda May. Her daughter, Ally, was the first and only best friend I'd had. Unfortunately, that friendship, like all things, came with an expiry date. But we'll get to that later.

Right now, I have a date with another friend. Or at least the closest thing I've got to one. I've never actually met the guy. I haven't a clue what he looks like, and I don't even know his real name. We found each other a couple of years ago in *The Shadow Realm of Lost Souls*, an online fantasy role-playing game.

I know, I know. It sounds hella nerdy, and it is. But it's also freakin' awesome! Plus, it's the only way I can make friends without being confronted with a huge number-imprinted elephant.

My online bestie's username is PrettyFly4aWhiteGuy98. But everyone calls him Fly because his profile pic is Jeff Goldblum, mid-mutation, in David Cronenberg's '80s classic, *The Fly*. He's the most skilled gamer I know.

This friendship is probably sounding less and less credible. But we message every day. In fact, that's him buzzing in my pocket right now. He just texted to inform me that the Emerald Forest of Forgotten Dreams is being invaded by axe-wielding ninja gnomes! Gotta run — we've got a forest to save.

CHAPTER THREE

STAND BY ME — BEN E. KING

Peace has been restored to the Emerald Forest of Forgotten Dreams. Every last ninja gnome has been obliterated! Fly and I stayed up until 2 a.m. exterminating the mischievous little devils. It was an epic night.

I've been working up the courage to ask Fly if he'd like to meet up. Like, in real life. But I keep chickening out. Thank god for social media. It gets a bad rep but I'd be lost without it. I'm more confident online. In person, my lack of social skills always makes things awkward.

But I know I've gotta get over that if I plan on getting a life this summer. I'm just terrified of losing the one friend I've got. It didn't end well the last time I got close to someone. Honestly, I'm still not fully over it . . . and I was 12.

Her name was Ally May, and she was the best friend I've ever had. Our mothers were like chalk and cheese — a classic case of opposites attract. I guess you could say the same about me and Ally. Mom bumped into Gilda on her way out of her grief counsellor's office. I guess they had the same one, and they quickly became inseparable.

Mom and I are textbook introverts, whereas Gilda and Ally were *extra* in every way. I think we needed that. Our house was too quiet without Dad, and we could always count on those two to fill the silence. Despite our differences, we all shared one morbid commonality.

I often wondered if Mom and Gilda would've been friends if they weren't widows. They were an odd pair of socks. Mom looked frail after Dad died. She began wearing drab clothes that were way too big for her and stopped wearing makeup after the funeral. Her greying hair had grown long and lifeless. It was as though grief was literally draining the colour from her body. Gilda, on the other hand, wore uncomfortably tight-looking clothes with loud prints and bright colours. She had red curly hair that she always wore in an elaborate updo. As if this wasn't flamboyant enough, she also looked like a cosmetic bag had exploded in her face. Ally often made jokes about how long it had taken Gilda to put her latest ensemble together.

Gilda was high-energy, a whirlwind of positivity and giggles. I found this creepy at first. *No one is that happy all the time*, I often thought. Especially after their husband just died. Then Ally told me she heard Gilda cry herself to sleep every night, and I felt like an asshole for judging her. It must've been a full-time job hiding her grief behind that peppy persona. It was Gilda's way of coping and protecting her daughter. I respect that in hindsight. She was a nice lady. She called everyone sweetie and always left a big lipstick kiss on your cheek as she greeted you.

Ally was her polar opposite. Much to her mother's dismay, Ally was a tomboy through and through. She reminded me of those scrappy puppies that try desperately to look fierce. No matter how loud she barked, she was a big softie deep down. Don't get me wrong, though — the girl was tough. She could kick my ass at just about every sport and video game going.

Ally didn't mind that I didn't make eye contact or talk a bunch. She talked enough for the both of us. She didn't even make fun of my sunglasses. She took people as they were. I loved that about her. It's a rare quality.

Ally's dad was a farmer, and she wanted to be just like him. The farm was all she talked about most days.

After he died, Gilda didn't have a clue how to run the place. She was a city gal with no interest in any of that mud. Her words. But Ally lived for it. The muddier the better.

She'd run home after school every day to muck out stables and feed the animals. But she was only a kid, and the farm was falling apart. Still, that didn't stop her from trying to fill her dad's muddy boots. She was stubborn that way. I think keeping the farm running was her way of honouring his memory. I often caught her talking to herself while doing chores around the rickety old place. I'm certain she was talking to her dad. But I never asked her about it.

Ally frequently asked questions about my dad. I didn't mind. Honestly, it was refreshing. Nobody talked about him after he died. Most people acted like he never existed. I understand they were only trying to spare my feelings. But I hated it. So it was nice having someone around who knew exactly what I was going through. I never told her so, mostly out of fear I'd get a smack in the mouth, but I thought Ally was the coolest girl in the world.

She had dirty-blonde hair that fell just above her jawline. Her bangs were always a little too long. I remember because she was constantly blowing them out of her face. She had a dark tan and freckles, as she spent more time outdoors than inside. She was happiest covered in dirt, hanging out of a tree. She was also full of wild ideas. When Ally had a plan, there was no talking her down. Come hell or high water, she never gave up until she'd given it everything she had.

Like the time she decided we should run away — to Alaska. Batshit, I know, but I'll never forget our adventure.

It was a clear blue morning in late spring — the kind of morning that lured you outdoors. Mom and I were having breakfast in the garden. We ate in silence as sunshine and birdsong worked its restorative magic. Until a shrieking telephone interrupted.

It was Gilda telling Mom that Ally and I had arranged a sleepover at our house that weekend. This was news to me. According to Ally, there was going to be a huge meteor shower and it was imperative she sleep over at my place that night. Apparently, we'd been planning it for weeks. This was also news to me. I figured she probably just needed a break from Gilda. Her mom was dating a new guy named Todd, and this had further strained their already tempestuous relationship.

Early that afternoon, their car pulled into our driveway. Ally jumped out before Gilda had even finished parking. She lugged an enormous rucksack over her shoulder and comically swayed back and forth under the weight of it. She barely made it to our front door without falling over.

'Oh my, are you moving in, Ally?' Mom asked.

Ally shuffled passed like she was in a hurry. 'It's just my telescope.'

Something was up. She looked shiftier than usual.

'Ah yes, the big meteor shower,' Mom replied.

'She's been squawking about it all morning,' Gilda said irritably, catching up with her wayward daughter. 'You'd swear it was the end of the world! But it's the first I've heard of any meteors in Fairview.'

'Are you a member of the Fairview Astronomy Club?' Ally asked in faux curiosity. She'd convinced me to sign up to the local astronomy club with her a few weeks earlier.

'No, I suppose I'm not,' Gilda replied.

'Well, that would explain why you haven't heard about it.'

Ally was the politest smart-ass I'd ever met.

She proceeded to drag her monstrous bag upstairs. I helped by pushing the weighty beast from behind. There was more than a telescope inside, that was for sure. The thing weighed a ton.

Meanwhile, Gilda was warning Mom that Ally wasn't always easy to handle. 'Lynn, give me a call if there's any trouble. Alison isn't like your sweet Theodore. She's a little more . . . *rambunctious*.'

Ally shut my bedroom door behind us.

'What time is this meteor shower?' I asked. 'I don't

remember hearing anything about it at astronomy club.'

Ally glared at me like I was a complete imbecile. 'There is no meteor shower, doofus.'

'I knew it! What are you scheming now?'

'Isn't it obvious? Your mom was right — I'm moving in.' She flung her arms in the air and pretended to faint on top of my bed. 'Because I'm madly in love with you, Theodore.'

I made an audible gulp.

'Barf! You wish, Brown. You're as gullible as our moms.'

'Very funny. Now spill it. What's really going on?'

'Can you keep a secret?' she whispered.

'Depends on the secret.'

'I'm not telling you until you promise, dingus!'

'Fine, I promise.'

She dropped to the floor and unzipped the front pouch of her rucksack. She proceeded to pull out a map of America, a compass and a jar of money. 'I'm moving to Alaska!'

This was unexpected, to say the least. Ally was full of wild notions. But this was bonkers even by her standards.

'What?' I didn't know what else to say.

'I know you ain't deaf, Theo. So either you're an idiot or you like making me repeat myself.'

'How're you gonna make it to Alaska, smart-ass? It's like a gazillion miles away.'

It's approximately 2,986 miles away from Fairview by car, which may as well have been a gazillion miles for the two of us on foot.

'Easy.' Ally shrugged. 'We just follow the map and pitch our tent each night. It'll probably take a few weeks, but the journey is half the fun.'

One word pierced my ears.

'We?'

'Whoops! I was supposed to give my *Hail Mighty Alaska!* speech first.'

'Ally, you barely made it to my bedroom with that bag.'

'Which is precisely why I need you. It won't be so bad when we split the load.'

'Gee, thanks. Find another bag boy. I'll pass!'

'Come on, I didn't mean it like that.' She pressed her palms together and pleaded, 'I can't do this without you.'

'What about our moms? What about school? You haven't thought this through.'

This didn't go down well. Ally looked like she was about to detonate.

'*Hello*! I live with Gilda! I knew it would come to this eventually. The woman makes Sideshow Bob look well adjusted!'

'What about *my* mom? She needs me. I can't just leave her.'

'Why? You two are miserable. You don't even talk to each other.'

'*That's not true!*'

This pinched, because it sort of was true at the time.

'Sorry, that was harsh,' Ally said. 'But I can't stay here. Please, trust me.' Her voice broke as she sank to the floor.

I didn't know what was wrong. But she was scared, and Ally rarely showed a hint of vulnerability. So when she did, I paid attention.

'Can you at least tell me what's up?'

'Not right now. But it's bad. I've gotta get outta here . . . and it would be way less terrifying if I had my best friend with me.'

This was the first time I'd seen Ally cry. It was also the first time anyone had referred to me as their best friend. I knew not to push. She'd tell me what was going on when she was ready.

'Okay, I'm in,' I said. I couldn't let her wander into the wilderness by herself. Besides, there was no way in hell we'd make it to Alaska. I just had to ride this out until she came to the same conclusion.

'You mean it?' she beamed, wiping her tears with her sleeve.

'As long as you promise not to get us killed?'

She sprang to her feet, gripping me in a bear hug. 'You ain't so dumb after all, Brown.'

'I'm not so sure about that anymore,' I replied, realising what I'd agreed to.

'Don't be a worry wart. It's gonna be the adventure of a lifetime — no more rules or curfews, just two best friends and the great outdoors.'

'What could possibly go wrong?' I replied.

Ally stood on top of my bed, placing her hands on her hips like Wonder Woman. 'Our grandkids will tell stories about our epic quest.'

'If we live to have any. How exactly are we gonna pull this off?'

She grinned as she unzipped the main compartment of her rucksack. Inside she'd packed a tent, sleeping bags, two large flasks of water and a shopping bag full of protein bars and potato chips.

'I've been saving my allowance for weeks. We can top up our food and water along the way. I've circled all the gas stations on the map. We might be able to hitch a ride some of the way, but that's risky. Most drivers would probably take us back to our parents.'

'Or worse. Ever heard of *stranger danger*?' I asked.

'Good point. It'll be more fun on foot anyway.'

'Wait, aren't you forgetting something? There's no way border security will let us through Canada without an adult.'

'No shit, Einstein. We're not going through the front door — we're taking a little *shortcut.*'

'And say by some miracle we make it to Alaska — what then?'

'We build a treehouse,' Ally replied nonchalantly. 'I can teach you how to hunt and fish. Like my dad showed me. He even taught me how to watch out for bears. Plus, I know which plants and berries are safe to eat.'

Nothing registered after *bears*. I'd seen the Discovery Channel. I didn't wanna get my face ripped off. Then I remembered how ridiculous this whole thing was. We'd be home by supper. I was sure of it. So, I grabbed my rucksack from my closet and split Ally's supplies between the two packs.

We snuck out as Gilda chatted up a storm with Mom in the kitchen. I wanted to grab extra food but it was too dicey. I'm a terrible liar, and Mom has Sherlock-level detective skills.

It was after 2 p.m. by the time we hopped over the fence at the end of Fairview's town park. It leads directly into the woods. The sun was shining, and Ally seemed confident she knew where she was going.

Ally was a different person in the wild. It was like nature melted away all that defensive bullshit she hid behind. She was light on her feet. I, on the other hand, was a fish out of water. I was content in my bedroom with my books, video games and a fully stocked kitchen downstairs.

'We'll keep going straight for another hour,' she said, holding the map in one hand and compass in the other. 'Then we gotta practise pitching the tent before dark.'

'Aye, aye, Captain.'

It would've been much easier with Google Maps. But thanks to Dr Phil and his special about online addiction, our moms had said we couldn't have phones until we were 16.

We shrank as the trees grew taller around us. The sun trickled through the leaves, creating intricate webs of golden light. Ally whistled the tune of Ben E. King's 'Stand By Me', and I prayed our adventure wouldn't turn out like the chilling Stephen King adaptation of the same name.

After an hour of walking, the magic began to wear off. I hit the ground like a sack of potatoes. 'Is it time for dinner?'

'Not yet.'

My stomach growled on cue. 'But I'm starving.'

'Just a little further. We can pitch the tent and eat soon.'

'Can't we pitch it now?'

'We haven't made enough ground. We'll be out here for months at this rate, and we gotta make our supplies last.'

'Mom is cooking meatloaf for dinner.'

'Meatloaf-Smeatloaf,' she sneered. 'When we get to Alaska, we can make our own meatloaf — with venison.'

'Oh yeah, how you gonna kill a deer?'

Ally grinned darkly. I knew that grin. Nothing good ever followed that grin. At best, it was accompanied by a lethal fart. At worst . . . well, you'll see.

'Don't freak out, okay?' she said coyly.

'What've you done?'

She reached into her bag and pulled out a balled-up sweater.

'You planning on strangling the deer with your sweater?' I asked. 'Good luck — those things are faster than horses.'

'No, dingus!' She unwrapped the sweater, revealing one of her dad's old pistols.

'ARE YOU FUCKING CRAZY?!'

I didn't swear much then. This was the exception.

'Calm down! It's not even loaded yet.'

'*Yet?*'

'It's not a big deal. My dad used to shoot cans with it. He even let me fire it once.'

'What the hell, Al?' She'd gone too far this time.

'I knew you'd freak. That's why I didn't tell you.'

'You gotta get rid of it.'

'No way! It was my dad's!' she huffed.

'And you really think he'd want you firing it?'

She hung her head and kicked at the dirt. She

obviously knew I was right. Her dad would've been pissed!

'We're gonna need meat. We can't fish in winter when the water freezes over.'

I remembered this was real for her. She really believed we'd make it to Alaska.

'We'll worry about that when the time comes.'

'But—'

'It's the gun or me, Al,' I said. 'No ifs, ands or buts.'

I hated how much I sounded like my mother.

'Fine. But what are we gonna do with it? We can't just leave it here.'

'We'll bury it,' I said.

I got on my knees and frantically clawed at the dirt like a dog. To my surprise, Ally didn't protest. But she didn't help me dig either. I buried the pistol, covered it back over, and we stood by its grave in silence. It was like we'd buried another piece of her dad.

I squeezed her shoulder in a feeble attempt to comfort her. 'He'd be proud. You did the right thing.'

She swatted my hand away like a bug. 'He would've been prouder if I'd caught us a deer.'

'Could you honestly shoot a deer?'

'If I was hungry enough.'

Ally loved animals. I don't believe she could've shot one. But I was glad the gun was gone and I'd never have to find out.

She marched on without looking back. 'Let's get moving. We've wasted enough time.'

I followed like a loyal lapdog, praying there were no more surprises in her bag.

There's something healing about the woods. The tension between us evaporated as we walked. Neither of us spoke for a long time. Until my stomach erupted with another loud gurgle.

'What kind of protein bars you got?'

'What don't I got?' Ally boasted. 'Double-choc, cookie-cream, banoffee, strawberry shortcake. You name it, I got it! Don't worry, I grabbed plenty of vanilla swirl for you.'

I sensed a dig. 'What's that supposed to mean?'

'Nothing,' she replied in a tone identical to Gilda's when she'd called Ally rambunctious. 'You're a boy of simple taste. There's no shame in that.'

'Whatever. Those things all taste like playdough anyway,' I sniped. 'They're not even real food.'

'What're you talking about? They're literally super-food.'

'Super-gross,' I teased.

'I'm sorry, precious. We'll get you some caviar at the next gas station.'

'Because gas stations are renowned for their caviar.'

She rolled her eyes. 'Shut up!'

We exploded with laughter, and Ally threw a banoffee

protein bar at my head.

I threw it back. 'Can you pass me a vanilla swirl?'

'Ha! I knew it!' she taunted.

The protein bars were terrible. But we sat under the shade of an oak tree and choked them down with some lukewarm water. I still think of Ally every time I see one. I'm sure she didn't like them either. I think she ate them because her dad used to chew on them while he worked on the farm.

After what felt like a lifetime of more walking, we came across a tree identical to one I'd seen earlier. I remembered because it had a distinctive bulge in its trunk that made the tree look like it was pregnant.

'Haven't we been here before?'

Ally scratched her head. 'No, everything starts to look the same out here after a while.'

'I dunno, Al, I'm getting major déjà vu. You sure the compass is working?'

Ally's cheeks turned fuchsia, and I noticed she wasn't holding the compass anymore.

'Al . . . where's the compass?'

'I dunno,' she said meekly.

'*What?*'

'I must've lost it when we stopped to eat. So it's not totally my fault. If your tummy wasn't so loud—'

'Please tell me you know the way home?'

'Home? We can't give up at the first hurdle.'

I threw my hands in the air. 'This is crazy! We're walking in circles.'

Ally crossed her arms and dug her heels into the dirt. 'You can go if you want. I'm staying.'

'How can you be so selfish? Our moms are gonna be worried sick!'

Ally scowled like she'd been slapped across the face. 'They're the selfish ones,' she squealed. 'And they can go to hell for all I care!' The words burst out in a fit of tears.

I couldn't stay angry with her. 'Al, Gilda loves you. No matter what she's done — she's still your mom.'

She dropped to her knees. 'If she loved me, she wouldn't keep taking him away from me!'

As usual, this wasn't about Gilda at all. It was about her dad.

'Gilda didn't take your dad away,' I said gently, sitting down next to her. 'His heart gave out. It sucks! Trust me, I know. But it's nobody's fault.'

'If she loved him, why's she trying to erase him?' she asked tearfully. 'First, she moved all his stuff into the basement. Not that there was much left — she donated all his clothes to charity without even telling me. She even took all his pictures down! And now—'

She couldn't finish her sentence. She was crying so hard she started to hyperventilate. I rubbed her back and told her to breathe. She steadied herself enough to finish her sentence.

'She's selling the farm, Theo! We're moving away. For good!'

A lump formed in my throat. I couldn't speak. I was so shaken by Ally's revelation; I looked her dead in the eyes.

27 DAYS!

I was flabbergasted. I hugged Ally tight and promised myself I wouldn't let anything happen to her. I'd unknowingly watched Dad zero out. But I knew the score this time. I'd find a way to protect her. No matter what. As far as I was concerned, that number could go to hell!

'I have nothing left of him,' Ally sobbed. 'He's gone. He's really gone.'

She fell apart in my arms. I didn't ask her to calm down. She needed to let it out. She'd held it in long enough.

'I know, I know,' I whispered, rocking her back and forth.

I was crying now too because I knew exactly how she felt. Our dads were gone, and that sucked beyond measure. But we were still here. And, thankfully, we had each other.

It's funny how weightless you feel after a good cry. It's like all the tension and pain comes flooding out in violent convulsions. Until there's nothing left. Then, for a brief moment, everything is still. You can breathe again. The catharsis is almost euphoric. But it never lasts. Life continues to shit on you. Until the cycle repeats.

It was getting dark by the time we finished our little trip down bereavement lane. So we pitched the tent and put our sleeping bags on a patch of grass so we could watch the night sky. The moon was full. It lit up the woods like our own personal night light.

We slept like two rocks under a sea of stars. I love sleeping under the night sky. It makes me feel small — in a good way. Because if I'm small, then my problems are small too. But all the stars in the galaxy couldn't shrink this problem. This felt overwhelmingly colossal, and I only had 27 days to figure it out!

CHAPTER FOUR

SUMMERTIME SADNESS — LANA DEL REY

Going to sleep in the woods is substantially more pleasant than waking up in them. We were torn from our starry woodland slumber by the harsh light of day. My throat was drier than the Sahara and I was dizzy with hunger. I could tell Ally felt embarrassed about crying. But I didn't bring it up. I knew she'd prefer it that way.

'Lead the way, Dora. Alaska ain't gonna explore itself,' I said, trying to sound optimistic.

Ally sniggered before punching my arm. 'Alaska will have to wait. Let's go home, nerd.'

'You sure?' I asked.

'I'm sure. You look like you're ready to eat a squirrel.'

I gave her a gentle shoulder-bump. 'Only if you're cooking.'

'That's all I'm cooking,' Ally said as she farted loudly.

'I'll pass, thanks.'

'You sure? It's high in sulphur.'

'You need to see a doctor!'

'We gotta get home first,' she replied. 'Come on, let's get the tent down and pack up.'

'Which way's home again?' I asked as I stowed away the last of my belongings and scanned the never-ending fields for any sign of civilisation.

Ally strode off confidently. 'This way.'

'How do you know?'

She shrugged. 'Just a hunch.'

I took a deep breath and hoped for the best. Ally's hunch was better than anything I had. Besides, she always managed to get us out of whatever scrape she'd got us into.

'How mad do you think our moms will be?' I asked.

'They'll get over it. If Gilda can haul me off to San Francisco against my will, the least she can do is call it even.'

I ground to a halt. 'San Francisco?'

'That's why she's selling the farm. She's moving there with Todd.'

They literally couldn't have put more distance between us. San Fran may as well have been Mars.

'When?'

'Bout a month.'

I grabbed Ally by the shoulders and stared into her eyes: 26 days. The countdown had begun.

'Jeez, Brown!' She wriggled free. 'Ever heard of personal space?'

I had a bad feeling. *What if their plane crashed? What if Todd wasn't as vanilla as he seemed? What if he was the next Ted Bundy?* My mind spiralled with endless possibilities, each more horrific than the last.

'But they've only just met!' I protested.

They'd actually been dating for over a year. Gilda had had a string of shortlived romances after her husband died. We figured this one would fizzle out like the others. But Todd hung around like one of Ally's farts.

It's safe to say Ally wasn't Todd's biggest fan. He seemed like a good guy, but he was nothing like her father. No one could fill those boots. Todd was a pretty boy who spent as much time preening his hair as Gilda did.

'Why can't Todd move into the farm?'

'Please.' Ally waved dismissively. 'That man's never broken a nail. The farm would chew him up and spit him out quicker than he'd say "chop, chop, lollipop!"'

This was one of Todd's frequent catchphrases. The guy made Ned Flanders look edgy.

'We'll find a way to stop them!'

Ally stuck her pinky out. 'Promise?'

I curled my pinky firmly around hers, and we marched on.

I had no idea how I was going to keep this promise. But I knew I couldn't do it alone. We were kids and this was adult territory. I'd need Mom's help, and that meant I would have to come clean and tell her about the numbers. I hadn't brought them up since Dad died. She'd thought I was talking nonsense back then. Now that I was older, I hoped she'd take me seriously.

We walked for what felt like hours. It wasn't even summer, but the sun was merciless. Our thirst quickly overtook our hunger.

'I don't know how much longer I can walk!' I gasped.

'It can't be much further.'

Ally fashioned her fingers into binoculars and scanned the perimeter. 'Over there!'

I squinted until I saw something glinting in the sun. I wasn't sure what it was, but we took off through the grass, hoping it wasn't a mirage. Thankfully, our eyes hadn't deceived us. It was a long wire fence.

Ally grinned. 'That's gotta be protecting someone's property. We must be near the motorway!'

'You think it's electric?' I asked as we approached.

Ally smirked. 'Only one way to find out.' She hovered her fingers over the wire. 'You dare me?'

'Don't be a dick!'

'You scared?' she teased, inching her fingers closer to the wire.

'Fine. Be a dick! Fry yourself!'

With no further warning, she grabbed the wire with both hands. I winced in horror as her whole body jerked violently.

'*Ally!*'

She crumpled to the ground in a lifeless heap.

I rushed to her side. 'Get up! This isn't funny.'

I tugged on her sleeve, but she didn't budge. 'Get up!' I pleaded. 'You can't be gone. We still have 26 days.'

She sprang to life in a fit of giggles.

'What is wrong with you?' I howled.

'It was just a joke! Don't go postal.'

'I thought you were dead! Don't ever do that again!'

'Chill!' She threw her hands in the air. 'What was all that about 26 days?'

I turned away. 'I just meant we don't have time to mess around. We've gotta figure out how to stop your mom from selling the farm.'

'That's an oddly specific number, though?'

Luckily, she didn't have time to quiz me further. I was saved by the bell. And by bell, I mean loud yelling.

'They're over here!' a male voice boomed.

We almost shot out of our shoes. Mom and Gilda were sprinting towards us like two wild gazelles. Behind them stood a police officer and what looked like half the neighbourhood. The next five minutes were a blur of kisses and threats. Tears streamed down our mother's faces as they simultaneously thanked the heavens and doled out punishments.

'Good thing you guys were making such a ruckus,' the police officer said. 'These situations don't always have a happy ending. You best take a good look at what you've done to your poor mothers.'

'Yes, sir,' we said in unison.

The four of us rode home together in the police car. Ally thought this was the coolest thing ever. I was too concerned about how long we might be grounded to enjoy it. It was an embarrassingly short car ride, proving we never stood a chance of getting out of Fairview.

Our house was the first stop on the way. I apologised profusely to Gilda and Mom again before I got out. We had a lot of buttering-up to do.

'Thank you, Theodore,' Gilda said. 'But I suspect you had little to do with concocting this scheme.'

'See you tomorrow, suck-up,' Ally teased.

'Oh, no you won't,' Gilda said. 'You're both grounded for the rest of your lives.'

Ally huffed and puffed. But I'd figured as much,

and I wasn't gonna kick up a fuss in front of a police officer. We had to be smart if we were gonna wrestle our way out of this one.

I looked in Gilda's eyes before I left. Her number was the same as Ally's.

THE 60-SECOND WALK UP our driveway felt like an eternity. My mind spiralled as I tried to find the right words to explain the numbers to Mom. I'd done everything I could to avoid stressing her out since Dad died. This included keeping my numeric nightmare bottled. But it was time to let the genie out. I was terrible at pretending to be well adjusted anyway.

The house seemed quieter than usual as we shut the door behind us. I didn't know whether Mom was ready to start yelling or crying.

'Before you get mad, I need to tell you something,' I said shakily.

'Oh honey, I think I know what this is about.'

Honey? I'd braced myself for an earbashing, not terms of endearment.

'You do?' I asked.

'Of course. You don't want to lose your friend.'

For a split second, I thought Mom could see the numbers too.

'I'm going to miss Ally and Gilda as well. But we

can talk on the phone and write to each other. It might be fun having a pen pal in San Francisco.'

'How long have you known?' I growled.

'I only found out a few days ago, I swear.'

'When were you going to tell me?'

'Gilda and Todd are planning a special dinner at the farm next weekend.'

I could feel my bottom lip starting to quiver. 'We can't let them go!'

Mom wrapped her arms around me.

'Oh sweetie, I know it's hard.'

'You d-don't under-sta-sta-stand!' I was crying so hard now I could barely string a sentence together.

'Wouldn't a trip to San Francisco be cool?'

'They're not gonna make it. They're gonna die!'

'Theodore, why would you say such a thing?'

She attempted to make eye contact when I failed to answer. This only made matters worse. The last thing I needed was to be confronted with another number.

'I know you're upset, but you need to calm down. No one is going to die.'

I shut my eyes and covered my ears. 'Yes they will! The numbers don't lie!'

'Not this again!' She sighed. 'Honey, this isn't like what happened to your father.'

This only added fuel to the fire.

'*This isn't about Dad!*'

'Then what's it about? Nothing bad is going to happen.'

'Just listen to me,' I pleaded. 'They're leaving in 26 days, right?'

She paused as she did the math in her head. 'Sure — something like that.'

'No. Not something. Exactly. They're leaving in *exactly* 26 days! How could I know that?'

Mom shrugged. 'Perhaps Ally told you.'

'Except she didn't.' I took a deep breath. 'I don't know why or how it will happen, but if we don't do something, they're dead!'

'*That's enough, Theodore!*'

Mom hadn't raised her voice in a long time. I wasn't sure she still could.

'This is my fault,' she continued calmly. 'You need to talk to someone about this.'

'I am talking to someone. I'm talking to you.'

'You need to talk to a psychiatrist . . . a special doctor—'

'I know what a shrink is, Mom. I'm not an idiot.'

'Of course not, honey, but—'

'I'm not crazy! Why won't you believe me?' I stormed upstairs. '*I hate you!*'

I slammed my bedroom door as hard as I could. A framed picture of Dad crashed to the floor. The glass cracked but didn't shatter. I didn't mean what

I'd said. I was just mad. Mom always told me to be honest, yet every time I tried she acted like I was crazy. I mean, if my own mother didn't believe me, what hope did I have?

I got into bed and pulled the covers over my head. I was expecting Mom to come knocking. But she never did.

The next morning I woke to the smell of home-cooked pancakes. It felt like I'd been asleep for days. I wanted to hide under the covers forever. But I was starving. I plodded downstairs, following the mouth-watering aroma to the kitchen.

Mom smiled brightly as she flipped another pancake. 'Morning, sleepyhead. I was just about to call you for breakfast.'

It was as if nothing had happened. She was wearing a pink apron and building a tower of pancakes dripping in syrup. I rubbed my eyes when I saw the time on the clock behind her. 'But it's 11.30.'

'Then you're just in time for brunch. That's the best thing about pancakes. They're delicious any time of day.'

Something was off. She was way too chirpy.

'Aren't I late for school?'

Maybe Mondays didn't exist in this bizarro world.

'I rang the school and told them you weren't feeling well. You had quite the adventure this weekend. I figured you could use some rest.'

'Can you call back and tell them I'm feeling better?'

She raised an eyebrow. 'You want to go to school?'

I had to see Ally. Now that we were grounded, school was our only opportunity to hatch a plan.

Mom shook her head. 'Now I'm worried you might actually be sick.'

'We're learning about . . . earthquakes today,' I said, unconvincingly. 'I've gotta be prepared. Missing out on that kind of information could be fatal.'

'I see.' Mom nodded. 'And this has nothing to do with seeing Ally?'

I didn't have the energy to keep up the flimsy façade.

'You don't have to lie,' she said. 'You can go to school if you really want to. I'll even have a word with Gilda to see if she'll consider *ungrounding* Ally.'

'Really?'

I smelled a rat. This all seemed too good to be true.

'You two need to make the most of your last few weeks together. I'm sure Gilda will agree when she calms down.'

'What's this gonna cost me?' I asked.

Mom set the plate of pancakes on the table in front of me. 'For a start, these pancakes aren't going to eat themselves.'

I sat down and stuffed my face with fluffy, buttery, syrupy goodness. 'No problem,' I said between gulps.

'Not so fast, buddy! There's one more condition.'

She paused before taking a seat at the opposite end of the table. I didn't like the way she twiddled her thumbs. 'I've found a doctor.'

The sweet taste in my mouth quickly soured.

'His name is Dr Green and he's super-nice. He's worked with kids from all over—'

'I don't need a shrink!'

'If you still feel the same way after you've spoken with him, I won't make you see him again.' She reached across the table and held my hand. 'Please, just give it a shot. For me.'

I mulled it over. I didn't like it. But I was in no position to bargain.

'I only have to go once?' I confirmed.

'Unless you change your mind. Who knows, you might enjoy it?'

'I won't,' I said, 'but okay. For you.'

My mom thought I was crazy, and that stung. But it was a fair deal. I could bullshit my way through one lousy therapy session. Then I'd go back to pretending I was the nice normal boy everyone wanted me to be.

I tried another forkful of pancakes but I'd lost my appetite.

Mom played the radio on the drive to school. She sang along to Lana Del Rey. But all the smiling and singing in the world couldn't mask her sadness. I was overcome with guilt.

'Mom?'

'Yes?'

'I don't hate you.'

'I know.'

I looked out the window and took comfort in Lana's melancholic tone. She knew a thing or two about loneliness, and so did Mom. Weirdly, this made me feel less alone. There was a sense of belonging in our collective lonesomeness.

When I made it to class, Ally's desk was empty. What? I'd given up a Mom-approved day off school for nothing? I tried not to panic. Ally's epic showdown with Gilda probably made my homecoming seem like a typical night with the Brady Bunch.

But then Ally didn't show up to school for the rest of the week either. I rang her landline every afternoon when I got home. No one answered. Mom said we needed to give Gilda time to cool off. But we were running out of time. I was Robin to her Batman. I couldn't crack this case on my own.

When Ally finally showed up at school the following Monday morning, it was like nothing had happened. But something weird was going on. An entire week had passed, meaning her number should have changed from 26 to 18. But it hadn't! It was 25. It had only changed by one day! It was like our week apart didn't exist.

Had I been wrong about the numbers?

CHAPTER FIVE

(DON'T FEAR) THE REAPER — BLUE ÖYSTER CULT

The inconsistency of Ally's number sent me into a full-blown existential crisis. There was only so much my 12-year-old self could handle. And I'd reached my limit. Her number hadn't changed for an entire week, yet it started counting down again as soon as she returned to school. I racked my brain trying to figure out what was different.

Then, it clicked!

She hadn't been with me during that week. Her number hadn't changed because we hadn't seen each other . . .

So did that mean I was sucking the life out of her

like some sort of vampire? I choked on the thought. Because if that was true, I killed my dad! And eventually I'd kill everyone I got close to.

In retrospect, I didn't have a lot of evidence to support this unsettling new theory. But I couldn't risk endangering anyone else. There was only one solution: solitary confinement.

I locked myself in my bedroom, vowing never to come out again. I'd choose isolation over murder any day. Besides, it wouldn't be so bad. I had my TV, books, video games and a comfy bed. Best of all, Mom had recently moved Dad's record player into my room as a peace offering. What more did I need? There were plenty of people in the world who had it worse. I felt more alone when I was with other people anyway. It was only when I was around other people that I realised how disconnected I was. Sure, I'd have to use the bathroom or sneak food from the kitchen occasionally. But those were the only exceptions.

I decided to embrace my new life as a hermit crab wholeheartedly. Until I learned via the Discovery Channel that hermit crabs are social creatures. They're actually pretty playful and sleep in large groups. They even have their own bartering system for trading shells. This was a depressing discovery. Even hermit crabs had better social skills than I did.

But at least I had an excuse for choosing a life of solitude. The citizens of Fairview were safer without the Grim Reaper lurking in their midst. I just had to figure out how to get everyone off my back. I'd accepted my role as the town's eccentric recluse. Every place needs at least one. Otherwise, who would everyone talk about? But Mom was going to be my biggest hurdle. She was *constantly* checking in on me, and I knew I couldn't get away with playing sick forever. The woman was relentless. How many temperature checks and bowls of soup did one boy need? This so-called virus was a temporary fix that was getting more temporary by the minute.

She was driving me crazy. I'm talking Jack-Torrence-from-*The-Shining*-level crazy. I was ready to go full 'Here's Johnny!' when I heard a knock on my bedroom door for the tenth time in a two-hour period.

'*I don't need any more chicken soup, Mom!*'

'How about a chill pill?'

It wasn't my mother's voice this time.

'Get out of here, Al!'

Ally poked her head through the door. 'Rude! What's eating you?'

'*I mean it. Get lost!*'

'Jeez! Should I tell your mom to call an exorcist?'

That wasn't a bad idea. I'd been considering solar urticaria, also known as sun allergy, as a potential explanation for my reclusive behaviour, but demonic possession might be easier to pull off.

'I'm not in the mood. Go pester someone else for a change.'

This was harsh. But it had to be. Ally was nothing if not persistent. Being obnoxious was the only way I could get her to leave.

'Fine! I'll be gone for good soon anyway. So you won't have to worry about me *pestering* you ever again!'

The hurt in her voice stung. My heart sank further with each thud as she stomped down the stairs and slammed the front door behind her. I peered out my bedroom window and watched her disappear. I wanted to run after her. But it was better this way. I could live with her hating me if it meant she'd be safe.

A few seconds later there was another knock on my door. I plunged my head into my pillow and screamed.

'Theo, is everything all right? Ally left in a hurry.'

'It's fine, Mom. I just didn't wanna infect her.'

'Okay, that's smart. I'll let you rest.'

I didn't expect her to let it go so easily.

'And don't stay up too late playing video games. We have your appointment with Dr Green in the morning.'

I knew there was a catch.

I WOKE THE NEXT day to an increasingly familiar smell. I started to hate pancakes. *Way to ruin a good thing, Mom.*

I groaned when I remembered what the day had in store. Running away to Alaska didn't seem like such a bad idea anymore. But there'd be no kicking and screaming. I'd given my word and I always made good on a promise. My appointment with Dr Green would be my last hurrah: one final venture to the outside world before my life of permanent seclusion began.

I popped my sunglasses on and ate my breakfast like a *good boy*.

Mom patted me on the back. 'This is gonna be good for us, Theo.'

I know she was trying to be supportive. But it was triggering.

'I'm only going once,' I barked.

'Let's just see how it goes.'

I didn't like her sprightly tone, or what she was implying. We'd come to an agreement, and I was holding up my end.

'Not until you promise I don't have to go again!'

'For god's sake, Theo!' She slammed her hand on the table. 'Could you at least pretend to be open to this? We're trying to help you.'

'So, you and Dr Green are "we" now. When did that happen?'

'Just get in the car,' Mom sighed.

'Are you dating him now?'

'Don't be absurd!'

'Am I getting a new daddy, like Ally?'

'*Enough! Just get in the damn car!*'

I didn't push. I'd already gone too far. I marched out to the car in a huff, and neither of us said another word the whole way to Dr Green's office.

It was only when we arrived that I realised how nervous I was. The building had that sterile hospital vibe, and the corridors smelled of disinfectant. The floor was so shiny I could literally see my reflection in it. I felt grubby in comparison. I was afraid to touch anything in case I sullied it.

An overly cheerful secretary with a neat blonde bob greeted us outside Dr Green's room. She pointed to a big white door with a nameplate in the centre: Dr Green, Developmental Psychologist. She smiled politely and nodded towards a row of chairs by the door. 'Take a seat, please. Dr Green will be with you shortly.'

The second my butt hit the chair I began to panic. Anger had been a nice distraction during the car ride but now reality set in.

What if Dr Green thinks I'm crazy? What if I am crazy? Could they keep me here?

My palms started sweating. I tugged at the neckline of my sweater. Either it was getting tighter or my neck was swelling. But before I could make a run for it, the office door opened.

A short, balding man with glasses, a white shirt, a blue tie and formal suit pants was standing there. He was much older than I'd imagined. The way Mom had talked about him, I'd expected some corny children's TV presenter. You know, the kind that tries *way* too hard to stay hip with the kids but ends up looking like a total square by using prehistoric lingo. In some ways, that might've been less intimidating — amusing, if nothing else. But this guy looked stiffer than my school principal.

Just act normal, I told myself.

'You must be Theodore. It's nice to finally meet you. I've heard wonderful things.'

I highly doubted that.

'Likewise,' I replied, standing up to shake his hand.

I decided it was best to be courteous. But I didn't make eye contact.

Not missing a beat, he got down on his honkers so we were at eye level.

I quickly looked back over my right shoulder. He smelled like Old Spice and peppermint. I could still see him in my peripheral vision, swaying back and forth trying to meet my gaze. I jerked my head from side to side as if he was an exorcist splashing me with holy water. So much for looking normal.

'Interesting,' he concluded. 'Why don't you come

through to my office and we can have a little chat.'

Mom stayed where she was.

'Aren't you coming?' I sounded like a four-year-old being dropped off at preschool for the first time.

'I've already got to know your mom quite well over the phone,' Dr Green said. 'Today I'd like to learn more about you, Theodore.' I gulped as he shut the door behind us. 'Please, make yourself at home. There's no need to be nervous.'

I nodded respectfully without saying a word as I looked around his office. It was just as bright as the rest of the building. Thankfully, I was wearing my sunglasses.

The walls were painted pale yellow, and there was a large leafy potted plant in each corner. I guess it was meant to create a calming atmosphere, but it felt contrived. Everything was a little too neat. There was a colourful wooden kiddies' table in the centre of the room, with a stack of crisp white paper on top and a rainbow of crayons perfectly lined up. Dr Green must've caught me eyeing them.

'You like to draw?' he asked.

'Not really,' I replied, settling for the leather chair opposite his desk.

'Fair enough.' He sat behind his desk and cleaned his glasses with a handkerchief. 'So, what brings you here today?'

'Hasn't my mom already told you that?'

'We've talked about *her* concerns. But I'd like to know why you think you're here.'

'Because everyone thinks I'm a freak!'

He tilted his head. 'What makes you think that?'

I felt like a bug under a microscope. 'Because I'm different.'

'You look like a bright young man to me.'

I said I was different, not stupid.

I leaned back in my chair. 'Looks can be deceiving.'

'Yes, that's very true. But so can our outlook. Sometimes a change in perspective can work wonders. And for the record, I don't think you're a freak, Theodore.'

I crossed my arms. 'No offence, but you don't know me, doc.'

He held his palms in the air. 'True, but I'd like to.'

'Why, because my mom's paying you?'

'I'd genuinely like to help.'

'Thanks for the offer, but nobody can help me. I just wanna be left alone.'

'How do you know I can't help? You don't know me yet either.'

This was beginning to feel like a chess match. And I sucked at chess! Especially the verbal variety.

'You wouldn't believe me if I told you the truth,' I sneered.

'I *believe* this is very real to *you*.'

He sounded sincere. But I knew what he really meant.

'Isn't that a polite way of saying *it's all in my head*?'

He paused, perhaps realising he wasn't dealing with your average 12-year-old. I'm not saying I was remarkable, but I could always read the bullshit between the lines.

'Processing grief is extremely difficult. Our minds are hardwired to protect us from pain. But sometimes the coping mechanisms we develop can prevent us from truly healing.'

He was speaking to me like an equal now, and I appreciated it. But he wasn't equipped to deal with my truth.

'This isn't about my dad!' I said, more aggressively than I'd intended.

'Right, it's about *the numbers*. The ones you see in people's eyes. Tell me about them.' He sounded fascinated, like I was some rare specimen at the zoo. 'Do you see them in everyone's eyes, or only those whom you're close with?'

How much has Mom told this quack?

'What do you know about the numbers?'

'I know your mother is very worried about you.'

My face burned as blood rushed to my cheeks. 'Whatever, she doesn't know anything.'

'She knows you're struggling, and she's trying to help because she loves you.'

I shook my head. 'Then why won't she listen to me?'

'Perhaps she's afraid,' he said. 'The ability to predict death is a frightening concept.'

I didn't respond. He already knew too much, and he'd clearly decided I was a nut before I arrived.

'When did the numbers first appear?' he went on.

For a shrink, he wasn't great at reading the room. I was done with this interrogation.

'What does that matter?'

'Maybe if we figure out *why* they appeared, we can figure out how to make them *disappear*.'

'Look, I appreciate the effort, I really do. But you're wasting your time. I made it all up.'

I could tell he didn't buy this.

'And why would you do that?'

I scratched my head. 'For attention.'

'But I thought you wanted to be left alone?'

Touché. The old fart was quick. Still, it wasn't like he could force the truth out of me.

'What can I say? I'm a paradox.'

'Have I said something to upset you? Because that was never my intention. You're clearly a very intelligent young man, and I'm not here to judge you. I'm here to help if you'll let me. But I can only do that if you're completely honest.'

I realised I was being too hard on the guy. The

integrity in his voice pinched. I would have spilled the beans if I really thought he could help.

'I'm being honest. I made the whole thing up.'

He leaned closer. 'Then why don't you remove your sunglasses and tell me to my face.'

'No!' I growled through gritted teeth.

'What's the harm? You made the whole thing up.' It sounded like a taunt.

I was pissed. But I wasn't about to go all Medusa and kill the guy.

'I don't feel like it. Now, if you don't mind, I'd like my personal space back! Your halitosis is making me gag.'

I don't usually get this pissy. But you know what they say about cornering a scared animal.

'All righty, I think that's enough for today,' he replied.

'Really?' Nothing was ever that easy.

'Sure, unless you have anything else to add?'

'No, I'm good.' I was already on my feet, heading for the door.

'I just have one request before you go.'

My sneakers squeaked as they skidded to a halt. 'What?'

'I just want to take a quick look at your eyes.'

Aw, hell no!

'Don't worry, we don't have to make eye contact. It will only take a second. Then you're free to go.'

It was risky, but I really wanted to go home. So I agreed.

I sat back down in the leather chair and removed my sunglasses. He waved a tiny torch in my face and tilted my head from side to side. I felt like I was being probed. The light was blinding.

'Can you look up to the ceiling?'

I wriggled uncomfortably. 'Sure.'

I wasn't used to this level of close contact. Somewhere between the ceiling lights and the torch, I lost my bearings. Everything went fuzzy. When I regained my focus, I wasn't looking at the ceiling, I was staring directly into Dr Green's eyes.

'*No! Get away from me!*'

His eyes were totally empty. Aside from two tiny black zeros.

I swatted the torch out of his hand. It flew across the room as I ran to the door. I put my sunglasses back on and rushed to Mom, burying my head in her coat.

'It was an accident. I didn't mean to. I didn't mean to,' I cried over and over.

She begged me to calm down. But how could I? I believed I'd just signed another man's death warrant. I started to hyperventilate.

Everything after that is a daze. I vaguely remember Dr Green saying something about spectrums and medications and scribbling something onto a piece of paper, and Mom stopping at the pharmacy on the way home.

As soon as we got back, I retreated to my fortress of solitude. I was borderline catatonic. The whole appointment couldn't have gone worse.

To my surprise, Mom left me alone for the rest of the day. I put on an old record and curled up under the bed covers. Sometimes when I play Dad's records I feel like he's with me. I imagine how he felt when he first listened to that album and wonder if my favourite songs were his favourites too. That day was the first time I listened to *Sounds of Silence* by Simon & Garfunkel. I lay in bed and let the music carry me away.

CHAPTER SIX

JAGGED LITTLE PILL — ALANIS MORISSETTE

I started having the worst recurring dream after my appointment with Dr Green. And by dream I mean my own personal *Nightmare on Elm Street*. It was one of those dreams within a dream — the kind where you wake up inside the dream and don't realise you're still asleep. It always started the same . . .

I'm running for my life.

A freakishly tall man in a black suit and top hat is chasing me. He keeps yelling, 'Times up, Theodore!'

The tall man has clocks for eyes. The hands on the clocks spin at rapid speed until he corners me. Then the hands stop abruptly at 12. He grabs my shoulders and lifts me high into the air. Before I can scream, he opens his mouth and a wooden bird flies out between his jagged teeth.

'Cuckoo!' the bird screeches.

I shoot up from my pillow in a feverish frenzy. But I'm still in the dream. It's dark out and I can hear music playing downstairs. Classical, or something without lyrics. I follow the haunting melody to the living room. There are two familiar figures crouching in the centre of the room. They have their backs to me. But I know it's Dad and Ally.

'We're running out of time!' Ally says, pointing towards a large hourglass.

I edge closer. They're constructing some sort of wooden jigsaw puzzle. But the pieces are all wrong. They vary in size and none of them seem to fit together. They're clearly from completely different puzzles.

'Dad?'

I reach out to tap his shoulder. But before I make contact, the figure's neck twists with a horrible crack as he faces me. It's Dad all right! But his face is long and distorted, like every drop of life has been drained away. The eyes are the worst part. They're sunken and black, aside from a tiny white zero glowing in the centre of each.

'Hello, Reaper!' Dad grins. 'Come for the girl?'

Ally lets out a horrible shriek and her eyes turn black, then those same glowing white rings appear.

'Who's next, Killer?' Dad asks. 'Mom's in the kitchen. She's making pancakes.' He laughs wildly.

Right on cue, Mom walks in with a tall stack of pancakes. They look as though they're wriggling. As she moves closer, I realise it's because they're infested with maggots.

'I made enough for everyone,' Mom says, looking right at me. Then she shrieks like Ally. She drops the plate, and it smashes on the floor. The colour drains from her face. It becomes hollow like Dad's. Her eyes go dark as those ghostly zeros come into focus.

The hourglass explodes! And everyone starts to melt. Their flesh rapidly decays, until their bodies disintegrate entirely . . .

The first night I had that nightmare, my bed covers were so drenched in sweat I thought I might've had a *little accident*. But there was no time to check, or to psychoanalyse the horror show. Mom was calling me for breakfast. Thankfully, it wasn't pancakes. It was bacon. Salty, crunchy goodness with a hint of maple. I was still shaken. But hunger trumps fear. I splashed some water on my face and followed my growling tummy to the kitchen. I crept in like a timid mouse approaching a trap.

Mom hadn't spotted me yet. She was busy pouring a glass of juice. I greedily eyed the plate of bacon on the table. She'd also made eggs with bright gooey yolks and buttery toast on the side. I quietly filled a plate and began to tiptoe away.

'Not so fast, buddy!'

I froze on the spot.

'You can eat in your room if you're still feeling sick,' she said. 'But I need you to take these first.'

I heard a clink as she placed something down. I turned carefully, ensuring I didn't look directly at her. There was a tall glass of OJ and two small white pills on the table.

'What are those?' I asked.

'They're going to help you feel better.'

This was what she picked up at the pharmacy on the way home from our appointment with Dr Green. I felt betrayed and a little scared. Who knew what he'd prescribed after yesterday's meltdown?

'You're drugging me now?'

'I'm not going to force you to take them. But we've got to try something.'

'Right. And medicating me is much easier than listening to me.'

She let out a deep sigh. 'That's not fair.'

'You're right. None of this is fair! But if popping pills is the only way to get you off my back — *fine*!' I grabbed the pills and slugged them back with a gulp of juice. 'Happy?'

I slammed the glass back onto the table and stormed off to my room. I heard Mom crying but was too enraged to feel guilty.

HONESTLY, THE NEXT COUPLE of weeks are a blur. The days rolled by like I was stuck inside some tripped-out '80s montage. True, after a few days on the meds, all my worries vanished. But so did everything else . . .

Sure, I didn't stress about the numbers anymore. But I also didn't give a damn about school. Or food. Or books. Or music. Or Ally. Or even my mom. I knew it wasn't healthy, but I didn't think I had a choice and it felt good to have a break from being scared all the time.

A week later, I returned to school. Ally didn't approach me at first. I knew she was still mad with me for yelling at her. But her good nature eventually got the better of her. She couldn't help but intervene when the mean kids started making fun of me.

'Hey, zombie boy,' Andy Miller taunted. Abnormal movements and muscle stiffness were other fun side-effects of the medication. 'What ya got for lunch? Lemme guess . . . is it brains?'

Andy stretched his arms out and strode towards me slowly like Frankenstein. He grabbed me by the collar and shoved me against the lockers.

'Get your hands off him, butt breath!' Ally shouted, grabbing him and kicking his ass to the curb so hard it left skid marks.

Andy was a particularly nasty kid. He was one of those bullies with a finely tuned radar that alerted him to the faintest hint of vulnerability in a five-mile radius. Recess was prime time for guys like him. He'd been sticking notes on my back and shooting spitballs at me for days. To be honest, I barely noticed and I didn't care when I did. If anything, Ally's intervention stunned me more.

'Are you okay?' she asked.

'Peaches,' I replied.

'That kid's a real dickwad!' she said. 'Don't let him push you around.'

'I don't mind,' I murmured.

'What's up with you? You do kinda look like you're auditioning for *The Walking Dead*.'

'I like that show!'

Ally shook me. 'Seriously, are you on drugs?'

'It's medication. It's helping me.'

'Holy shitballs! I was joking. But you're actually high!'

'I should go,' I said. 'It's not safe for you to be around me.'

She didn't follow.

LATER THAT DAY, ALLY burst into my bedroom as I was attempting to finish my homework.

'Okay, junkie! Let's get you clean,' she said. 'Where's your stash?'

I rubbed my eyes. 'What're you talking about?'

'Your happy pills.' She placed her hands on her hips. 'Where they at?'

'Mom has them. Why?'

'Because it's flushing time!'

'No! I need them!'

'Theo, look at yourself.' She grabbed me by the shoulders. 'You're not okay.'

I stared her dead in the eyes. Her number had changed. It was down to 5. I'd totally lost track of time. I'd seen Ally every day at school but I was out of it. I hadn't noticed her number had got so low.

'I'm sorry,' I yelped.

She wrapped her arms around me. 'You have nothing to apologise for.'

The hug caught me off guard. She was warm, and for a brief moment I felt safe — until I remembered why I couldn't be close to her.

'Stay away. I'm bad, I'm bad,' I cried.

She gave me a firm shake. 'You're not bad! You're good. And sweet. And there is *nothing* wrong with you. *Nothing*.'

I pulled away as the reality of Ally's number sank in.

'I'm gonna fix this,' she said. 'Just promise you won't take any more of those pills.'

I didn't respond. I was sobbing too hard.

Ally stormed downstairs. She set off on my mom like a firework show on the fourth of July, and slammed the door hard when she left.

The house was eerily silent when I crept downstairs later that evening. I poked my head into each room until I found Mom sitting at the kitchen table. She looked like she hadn't slept in years. She took one look at me and burst into tears. I rushed to her side and hugged her.

'It's okay, Mom. I'm ready for my meds. Everything's all right.'

'No, it's not,' she sobbed. 'But it will be.'

She got up and grabbed my medication from the cupboard. 'No more pills. And no more Dr Green. I'm so sorry, sweetie.'

I winced as she flushed the pills down the garbage disposal. I knew it was for the best. But I was gonna miss not feeling anything.

The next few days were rough. School was the worst. Everything was loud. And bright. And obnoxious. But at least I still had Ally.

'You clean?' she asked, gingerly taking a seat next to me in class.

'Sure, I just had my annual shower.'

'You know what I mean.'

I rolled my eyes. 'Relax, I'm drug free.'

'Aren't you in withdrawal? Don't you have the shakes or cold sweats or something?' She sounded genuinely curious. 'Gilda made me watch this after-school special once and it was a real horror show.'

'I wasn't on heroin, Al!'

'You coulda fooled me!' She punched me on the arm. 'I missed you, dingus.'

'Missed you too, weirdo.' I forced a smile. 'But I'm back, and I ain't going nowhere. And neither are you. We still have a couple days to figure this out.'

Ally looked down at her desk and bit her bottom lip. She only did this when she wasn't telling me something. She didn't say much after that. I assumed this was because class had started. But she was quiet during lunch too. This was troubling. Ally was many things. *Quiet* wasn't one of them. But I told myself she'd perk up once we got brainstorming.

That night, our moms had arranged a sleepover. So much for being grounded. I think Gilda was feeling guilty about separating us. She dropped Ally at my place at around 5 p.m. and we headed straight up to my room. I locked the door behind us. I was keen to get cracking and had my whiteboard and markers ready. But Ally's lack of enthusiasm was obvious.

'Look,' I said, 'I know we don't have much time, but we can still pull this off. Let's throw as many ideas at the board as possible. Then we can separate the crazy from the slightly less crazy. I have a few ideas. But yours are always better. Hijacking your passports could buy us more time if you—'

'Theo, stop!'

'You're right, that's a rookie move. I knew you'd have something better.'

'I want to go,' Ally said. She spoke so softly, I thought I'd misheard.

'What?'

'I want to move to San Francisco.' She looked down awkwardly at her shoes. 'It actually looks sorta cool . . . Mom said Golden Gate Park is even bigger than Central Park, and there's this awesome fog named Karl, and it even has its own pet cemetery.'

'Sounds like a recipe for a Stephen King novel, and you know how those usually end — misery and death.'

'Don't be a jerk!'

'Then don't be dense,' I snapped. 'What about the farm?'

'The farm is falling apart.'

'So, you're just gonna walk away? What about all your dad's hard work? He built that place. It's his legacy.'

Ally sat on the bed and started sobbing. 'That's not fair. Don't use my own words against me.'

I knew I'd overstepped as soon as the words left my mouth.

'I'm sorry,' I said, and took a seat next to her.

'I don't wanna fight, Theo. I'm tired of fighting. And I'm tired of being angry all the time. I'm sick of arguing with my mom — hell, I'm even sick of giving

Todd a hard time. He ain't so bad, you know.'

'Okay, now I know you're tripping. Todd's a goober.'

'Yeah, but he's a good-hearted goober and he makes Gilda happy.'

'But what about us?'

'We can write — I've never had a pen pal. And you can visit.'

'Have you been brainwashed? You sound just like our moms.'

'Come on, it's not like we have a choice. We may as well look on the bright side.'

'You don't get it, Al. There is no bright side.'

She threw her arms in the air in frustration. 'Why are you being such an asshole? Can't you just be happy for me?'

'Because you aren't going to San Fran . . . and if you try . . . you'll die!'

She leapt off the bed. 'What the hell! Are you threatening me?'

I put my hands up and slowly moved towards her. 'I didn't mean it like that.'

She backed away, reaching for the door handle. 'You sound insane.'

'*I'm not crazy!*' Yelling wasn't the best way to diffuse the situation, but she'd touched a raw nerve.

'I should go.' She turned the door handle vigorously, forgetting I'd locked it.

'Please, calm down and listen . . . I'm trying to help you.'

'I don't want your help. I wanna go home.'

'Jeez, I'm not gonna hurt you. But if you leave . . . something terrible is gonna happen.'

'Let me out!' Ally cried.

'Fine!' I threw the key at her. 'Go die! See if I care!'

Obviously, I didn't mean this. But I couldn't stand watching her act like I was crazy. She was my best friend. Why was she, like everyone else, so quick to believe I was insane?

As soon as Ally got her hands on that key, she vanished faster than the Flash.

I locked the door behind her in case Mom came fishing for an explanation. I wasn't in the mood to talk. Then I grabbed one of Mom and Dad's old records and blasted it. Full volume. I was vibing hard with Alanis Morissette's *Jagged Little Pill* album at the time. I had no idea what the lyrics meant when I was 12. But I understood something about the fury that drove them.

SUFFICE IT TO SAY, the bon voyage dinner was an absolute shit show! Our moms' attempts to put a positive spin on the whole ordeal only made it more tragic. It was like a kid's birthday party that no one showed up to. Ally and I weren't even speaking. I was mad because she wouldn't give me a chance to explain myself and she was too afraid to even look at me.

The only person in the mood to party was Todd. He'd prepared a monstrous feast. There was a pyramid of burgers and hotdogs in the centre of the table. This whopping tower of cholesterol was surrounded by stacks of shiny brioche buns, curly fries, chicken drumsticks and an array of colourful condiments.

'Chop, chop, lollipop! Grab yourself a plate and tuck in!' Todd said, rubbing his hands together.

Neither Ally nor I budged. We sat, arms folded, scowling at each other as the adults filled their plates.

'You two are awfully quiet this evening,' Gilda said brightly. 'Not to worry, I have just the thing to fix that!' She reached under the table and took out two glittery gift bags. 'If this doesn't get you two talking, I don't know what will.'

'What do you say, Theodore?' Mom said.

'Thank you,' I obliged.

Ally's eyes widened as she tore through the wrapping and held out a brand-new iPhone. 'Wow! Thanks, Mom.' She must've been genuinely impressed, because she never referred to Gilda as Mom. This had been yet another source of contention between them.

'Go ahead.' Mom nodded. 'Open yours.'

'Whatever could it be?' I replied glumly, unwrapping the phone and plonking it on the table.

‘Isn’t that cool, honey?’ Mom squeezed my shoulder. ‘You’ll have to get Ally’s number before we go.’

I pushed the phone away roughly. The mention of Ally’s number was triggering. I knew Mom was talking about her phone number, but it stung all the same.

I looked across the table at Ally and my heart broke. Those wicked zeros had finally surfaced. Ally smiled half-heartedly as a peace offering. But it was too late.

I peeked at Gilda and Todd’s eyes too. Zeros across the board. Todd wasn’t a serial killer after all.

That was the moment I convinced myself their plane was going to crash. I jumped up and backed away from the table, knocking Todd’s chair so hard the wiener fell out of his hotdog bun.

I covered my eyes. ‘*Stop staring at me!*’

‘Honey, calm down.’ Mom inched towards me cautiously like I was a pet that had suddenly gone feral. ‘No one is staring.’

‘Come on, buddy,’ Todd offered. ‘Talk to us. How can we help?’

‘Talk to you! What’s the point? Nobody listens!’

‘Is it the phone?’ Gilda added. ‘Because they come in other colours.’

‘Jesus! It’s not about the phone. It’s not about my dad. And it’s not about you guys moving away!’

‘For heaven’s sake! Then what is it?’ Mom snapped.

'I've already told you, *Mother*. They're all going to die!'

Gilda's mouth dropped open, and Mom's face turned maroon.

'I'm so, so sorry about this,' Mom stammered. 'Thank you for a lovely meal, Todd.'

'Please, just listen!' I cried in a last-ditch attempt to get through to them.

But Mom was frantically packing our belongings. 'I think Theodore needs to get a good night's sleep. Thanks again for a lovely evening . . .' She grabbed me by the arm and dragged me towards the exit.

'DON'T GET ON THAT PLANE! IT'S NOT SAFE. YOU'LL DIE!'

I was carted off like someone on their way to a psychiatric facility. I kicked and screamed all the way to the car.

Ally cried her eyes out in the driveway as Gilda held her tight. Todd waved limply as we drove away.

That was the last time I saw Ally.

I hate that this is the final image I have of her. It's burned into my memory like a cruel punishment.

THE CAR RIDE HOME was not my proudest moment.

'*You're a murderer!*' I screamed. '*This is your fault, not mine!*'

Mom didn't respond. She went straight to bed as soon as we got back.

Next morning, she was nowhere to be found. She'd left to say goodbye to Gilda and for obvious reasons decided not to take me along.

There was nothing I could do anymore, but I couldn't just sit and wait for their obituaries to be printed. So I got on my bike and cycled frantically to the farmhouse. I pounded on the door until my knuckles hurt, but no one answered.

It was too late . . . They were gone.

I pushed my bike slowly back down the driveway. That was when I spotted the For Sale sign on the lawn. I smashed that sign into a million pieces.

I cycled for hours after that. I must've covered every square inch of Fairview, and on every inch I found a memory of Ally.

You don't realise how deep an imprint someone's made on your life until they're gone. It's only when they're nowhere to be found that they're suddenly everywhere . . . Ally was in the dirt we rode our bikes on. She was in the trees we climbed. She was in the grass we lay on and the clouds we stared up at. She was everywhere. Still is. Some people never truly leave you. They simply become a part of you after they've left.

After I'd worn my legs out on my bike, I retired

to Rocks Edge. It's a lookout point with a spectacular view of the whole town. It's also a popular make-out spot. Not that I knew from experience. It's just one of those facts kids have known since time immemorial. Ally and I had spent countless hours sitting up there, dreaming about the future. We'd gaze beyond Fairview and invent glamorously fictitious lives for ourselves. These daydreams weren't confined by dreary logic . . . we saw ourselves sipping on Pepsi in the swimming pools of our matching condos, waiting for our agents to call about our latest movie roles. We imagined some pretty cool shit, but sitting on that dusty old spot with Ally was just as cool to me.

I sprawled out on top of the rock and stared at the sky. I gazed in wonder as vibrant pink and orange swirls spun into deep-purple waves. When the clouds cleared, they unveiled a midnight-blue canvas glittering with stars.

Dad once told me that some of the stars are already dead. But we can still see them because they're so far away it takes years for their light to reach our eyes. I think people are like stars. Maybe it doesn't matter which ones are alive or dead. Maybe all that matters is the light they leave behind.

I fell asleep, comforted by this thought.

I was shivering with the cold when I woke. I had no idea how long I'd been asleep. It was still dark, so maybe it hadn't been too long, but I was stricken with guilt . . . Mom would be worried. Maybe she'd already heard the news . . .

Were they dead? Had the plane gone down?

Statistically, they were more likely to die in the car on the way to the airport. But plane crashes are infinitely more frightening.

I cycled home as fast as I could, picturing Mom's face as she got word. I didn't want her to be alone.

Mom was opening the door as soon as I parked my bike on the driveway.

'I'm sorry!' I cried. I'd never wanted to be right about any of this.

'Where have you been?' She threw her arms around me. 'I was about to call the police.'

'Sorry we couldn't save them,' I sobbed. 'It's not your fault.'

She wiped my tears away. 'Honey, nobody needs saving. Everyone is fine.'

'What do you mean?'

'I just got off the phone with Gilda. They made it to San Fran safe and sound.'

'But how? The numbers—'

'The numbers aren't real, sweetie. Call Ally and see for yourself. Your new phone is all set up.'

I sprinted inside and scanned the living room. The phone was sitting fully charged on the coffee table.

'What's Ally's number?' I hollered.

'It's already in there.'

I had no idea what to say. I was contacting either a ghost or someone who believed I'd lost the plot. Would she even respond after my bizarre encore? I was too afraid to call, so I sent a text instead.

Hi 😊

Original, I know. But I couldn't think of anything else to say. Besides, it didn't matter what I said. All that mattered was whether I got a response.

I came close to throwing up while I waited. Minutes felt like hours. Until finally . . . ping! There's never been a sweeter sound.

Hey Doofus!

That's all the first text said. But those were the best two words I'd ever read in my entire life. Then the phone pinged a second time.

R U OK?

Was I okay? I'd never been more okay in all my life! My best friend was alive. If I wasn't so athletically challenged, I would've been doing backflips.

We spent the rest of the night texting. I apologised for how weird I'd been acting and said it must've been a residual side-effect from the pills. This was bull, but Ally seemed to buy it.

We texted every day for a while. It wasn't the same as hanging out. But we'd never had phones before, so it took a while for the novelty to wear off. Besides, a virtual friend was better than a dead friend.

Mom and Gilda talked about visiting each other for years, but nothing was ever officially locked in and eventually we all drifted apart. Ally and I continued to talk, but our texts became less and less frequent as time passed. Life just happens that way sometimes. Our lives and interests changed so much, we couldn't relate anymore. I've kept tabs on Ally via social media over the years, though. Gilda and Todd got married, and Ally has two brothers now. She plays for a football team in San Francisco. She looks happy.

Losing Ally sucked major donkey balls at the time, but I'm still glad we met. I hate to admit it, but perhaps my therapist is right. Maybe it's time to let someone in . . . It'd be nice to have a friend like her again.

My time with Ally had another significant consequence. It took a few more zeros and several more years before I figured it out. But eventually I realised the numbers weren't necessarily a death sentence. They were simply counting down to the last day I'd see that person. In my dad's case, that was the day he died. In Ally's case, it was the day she moved away. This meant I wasn't to blame. I wasn't a Reaper after all.

CHAPTER SEVEN

HEY JUDE — WILSON PICKETT

I'm just back from my latest session with Dr Johnson. It feels weird calling him that. *Doctor Johnson* sounds so formal. He and I have a more casual set-up. I call him Hey-Jude, like the song. As always, there's a story . . .

When we first met, Dr Johnson asked me to call him by his first name, Jude. So, at the start of every session I'd say, 'Hey, Jude'. One day, he started singing in response. I thought he was making fun of me at first, until I realised he was singing the Beatles song. Personally, I prefer the Wilson Pickett cover. But it's become our thing. Now, even when I'm saying goodbye, I say, 'Bye, Hey-Jude.' It sounds weird now that I've explained it. I guess you had to be there.

Anyway, Hey-Jude is cool. He's not what I expected before I started therapy. I guess you could say he's *new-agey*. He's less about prescribing pills and more about breaking down emotional walls. That sounds 50 shades of corny. But it works. I'm much better since I started seeing him. He really listens, and he never makes me feel like I'm crazy. I get that he's just doing his job, but unlike some other doctors I've met, he takes that shit seriously. He doesn't throw random pill combinations at you until you leave his office smiling — doped up to your eyeballs. He genuinely cares.

That's rare these days. You don't often meet people who love what they do. It's kinda sad when you think about it. Sometimes, I look around and it's like everyone's on autopilot. I don't want to simply go through the motions, and I don't want to forget why I chose to be a writer. I want to be in it — present and engaged. Like Hey-Jude. I guess that's why I enjoy our sessions. Even though I bust his balls a lot, he gives me hope.

I STARTED SEEING HEY-JUDE about a year and a half ago. I was in a pretty dark place. *That* Theodore makes *present-day* Theodore look like Mary Poppins.

I was a total emo. I may as well have worn a T-shirt that read My Life Is a Black Abyss. I've never been much of a talker, but back then I literally spoke to nobody. I'd even iced Mom out. In my defence, teenagers can be nightmares under the best of circumstances, and I had a lot of extra shit on my plate. At 17, things reached boiling point. All the crap with the numbers, losing Dad, Ally moving away, my hopeless social skills — it was too much. Atop this mounting pile of trauma was the turbocharge of rampant teenage hormones. My pain was in 4K high definition and I simply couldn't take any more loss. So, I shut down.

I lost interest in all the things that used to give me comfort. I stopped reading, writing and playing video games. I became what I now refer to as Robo-Theo. I got up. Showered. Got dressed. Went to school. Did my homework. Ate dinner. And went to bed.

Wash. Rinse. Repeat.

I'd lost my appetite for life.

I wanted to die.

I know that's a heavy statement. But this is an important part of my story. And, unfortunately, that was my truth.

Still, according to the numbers, I wasn't going anywhere for a long time. You see, I knew the exact day I was going to die!

Even now, I don't just see a number in everybody else's eyes. I have one too. And I see it every time I look in the mirror. My number is currently sitting at 24,445

— which means I'm gonna live to the ripe old age of 86. At least I assume this is when I'll croak — it's not like I can break up with myself.

Most of the time, I'm okay with this. You could do a lot worse than 86. You could go at 33, like my dad.

My number drops consistently by one each day. This is what leads me to believe that my actions don't affect it. But when I was 17 that wasn't gonna stop me from trying. Then, I'd decided to take matters into my own hands — by any means necessary. Even if that meant ending my life.

Spoiler alert! I survive.

I hate when people say things like, 'Suicide is selfish.' Because, no offence, that's ignorant as fuck! Unless you've walked in someone's shoes and lived inside their head, who are you to pass judgement on their actions?

When you reach a point where you're considering ending your entire existence, you're not well. You believe you'd be doing everyone a favour by checking out. That's not selfish. That's mental illness. And I reckon we won't be able to treat this illness until we eradicate the stigma around it — stigma that we created. That's the real killer.

We've got to do better. We've got to get comfortable with uncomfortable conversations. Nothing will improve until we do. Yeah, yeah — I'm aware of the irony of me preaching the importance of communication. But even I've gotta let some air out occasionally. Repression is a temporary fix. You can only cram so much into that bottle before the glass shatters. I learned this the hard way.

For me, there wasn't one specific incident that triggered my feelings of wanting to end it all. It was an accumulation of grief and trauma during the most vulnerable period in my life. In other words, shit got way too real way too fast. I couldn't carry the load on my own any longer and I hadn't learned how to ask for help. I live in a small town and nobody was talking openly about things like anxiety or depression, not even at school, where you'd think it would be on the radar.

I can remember the very first time I thought about suicide. Not in a personal sense, in a more general capacity. It was just an ordinary day. Coulda been a Monday, coulda been a Thursday. I was sitting in math class. There was this one quadratic equation that had me stumped. I tried sneaking a peek at what the guy next to me was doing, but he seemed equally clueless. He must've caught me trying to mooch off his answer sheet, because he quickly turned to me and said, 'The solution is simple.'

'It is?' I said, watching as he ripped the page right out of his textbook.

'Sure,' he replied, scrunching the page into a ball

and firing it into the trash. 'Destroy the book! No math book — no math problems.'

We both laughed. It was just a throwaway joke. But he wasn't wrong, and it got me thinking about my personal problems. *No more Theodore. No more problems.* It sounds silly. But I think that's when the notion first crept into my head. I wasn't seriously contemplating suicide but I recognised it as a way out. The seed had been planted. And it grew like poison ivy, spreading to every crevice of my mind.

Several months later, I'd completely lost control of my mind. The poison had stolen my autonomy. Things had got so dark, I'd even set a date. One of Mom's old friends from high school was getting married in another town. Originally, Mom had hoped I'd tag along. But I told her she needed to get out more, and suggested she take a date as her plus one. She laughed and said I should take my own advice. Touché, Mom.

Looking back, I still wonder how I could have even considered putting my mom through more trauma. All I can say is that I believed wholeheartedly she'd be better off. My polluted mind convinced me that I was nothing more than a burden. With me out of the picture, she could start over. Meet a new guy. Maybe even have another kid — a normal one this time. I thought I was the reason she was sad.

I was supposed to be the man of the house. But I could barely fill my own shoes, let alone Dad's. The only features Dad passed down to me were physical. I have his thick black hair, his nose and his crooked smile. But I felt like an insult to his memory, undeserving of sharing his appearance. I imagined it was agonising for Mom to look at my sorry face every day and see a glimpse of him.

She'd be better off without me.

The world would be better off.

And my pain and loneliness would be over.

It's a win-win.

These were the putrid thoughts that stained my mind.

You see, it wasn't that I didn't care or because I was selfish. I was sick. So sick I didn't even realise it. I didn't have the confidence to talk to anyone about how I was feeling, and I had no clue how to ask for help. Boys don't cry, right?

Wrong!

My cries were deafening. I just didn't know how to vocalise them.

It's strange recollecting those thoughts. It's fucking horrible, to be honest.

Suicide is devastating. And scary. So, it's natural to want to look away. But to fight this thing, I couldn't hide under the covers and pretend it didn't exist. I had to dig deep, find my inner Buffy and face this demon head-on.

I felt dreadful the morning Mom left for the wedding. Not because of what I'd planned to do, but because of all the food that would go to waste. Mom had prepared all my meals for the three days she'd be away. Breakfast, lunch and dinner. She even labelled the containers. I told her I was old enough to cook for myself, but she insisted. I suppose she was afraid I'd eat nothing but cereal — which, to be honest, was a fair assumption. But I felt really guilty that I wouldn't be around to eat the meals she'd gone to a lot of bother to put together. This is a perfect example of how fried my mind was. To me, her pot pie and lasagna were worth more than my life.

My initial decision was that I would not leave a note. But now I felt like I had a reason to apologise. This is what I wrote:

I'm sorry Mom.
I put the food in the freezer.
It will still be good when you get home.
I love you.

Theodore

I GAVE MOM A big hug before she left. It must have surprised her, because I'll never forget how happy she looked.

'Maybe I should leave town more often,' she said.

A foreboding quiet filled the house as I shut the door behind her. There was a palpable finality in the air. I popped the food in the freezer and stuck my pitiful goodbye note to the fridge. I paced around aimlessly for an hour or so. I didn't know what to do with myself.

I decided against a last meal, because if this was gonna work I'd need an empty stomach. I'd spent many sleepless nights deciding how to do it. I didn't want to leave a huge mess, so I'd opted to overdose. But this was ridiculous. There's no clean way to kill yourself. No matter how you do it, the aftermath is going to be ugly, smelly and traumatic for the poor person who finds the body. I'd also given that aspect a lot of thought.

I didn't want Mom to be the one to find me, and I didn't want my body rotting up the house for days either. I wanted to ensure the body was taken care of immediately. It's gruesome. But someone had to find me. I ordered a pizza online and entered my address for delivery. Then I unlocked the front door and stuck another Post-it on the outside:

Pizza money is on the kitchen counter.
The body is upstairs.

Please call someone for disposal.
Sorry for the inconvenience.
Keep the change.

I went up to my bedroom, where I'd stashed pills and a bottle of whiskey I'd found in the back of a cupboard. I threw them all on the bed. I lay next to them for a moment, wanting to take everything in one last time. I examined the old movie posters on my walls . . . And the leaning towers of dusty paperbacks stacked in every corner . . . And the record collection I once treasured. All these things had meant so much to me once. Now it was as though they were never mine at all.

My eyes finally settled on Dad's record player. There was only one thing left to do . . . play one last song for the road.

I put on Cat Stevens's 'Father and Son' and knocked back the whiskey and pills. They burned like hell on the way down. But I lay back and let the music distract me. The melody washed over me like a cool wave on a summer's day. The album was Dad's favourite. He played it so much he wore out his first copy and had to buy another. I hadn't listened to it since he died. It was too painful. But if I was gonna choose one final song from it, it had to be this one.

But something unexpected happened when I dropped

the needle on that old record. The song I chose to end my life with ended up saving it.

Okay, that might be a slight exaggeration. The year-and-a-half of therapy that I've done with Hey-Jude has also helped a lot. But that song tapped into something buried deep inside. It pierced my very core. I believe it inspired me to seek the help I needed.

When I played that song, it was like Dad was home. He was in the kitchen cooking up a bacon breakfast. I could smell it and I could hear him singing along. It felt so real.

Sense memory is a powerful force. My entire childhood came flooding back as the song played! I was a happy kid, and my family loved me more than anything in the world. They wouldn't want this for me. Heck, I didn't want this for me. I can't fully explain it. It was like someone flipped a switch. The dark clouds that fogged my mind began to part. And as they cleared, I was bombarded with one overriding thought . . .

WHAT THE FUCK AM I DOING?

It's a bit of a blur after that, but I remember I raced to the bathroom, stuck my fingers down my throat and threw my guts up. I puked until I could puke no more. Years of pent-up emotion poured out of me in streams of barf, snot and tears. And when I'd got all of it out, I broke down sobbing on the cold bathroom tiles.

I couldn't believe what I'd almost done. I was both shocked and overcome with relief. For the first time in forever, I was grateful to be alive.

I went back to my bedroom and listened to the rest of the Cat Stevens record. I thought about Dad and all the things he'd never get a chance to do. He'd had such a lust for life. He didn't waste a single second he was given on this Earth. In that moment, I promised myself I wouldn't either. I couldn't give Dad more time. But I could honour him by making the most of mine.

I sat down at my desk, took out a notebook and pencil, and made a bucket list. I scribbled down everything I could think of that might be worth doing. My pencil could barely keep up. I listed all the countries I wanted to visit, foods I wanted to try, books I wanted to read and books I wanted to write. There was no dream too big or too small. I also listed a few more *personal goals*. I was still a virgin, for Christ's sake.

What had I been thinking?

My work here was far from over. I'd barely begun. There was no way in hell I was checking out early.

It probably sounds unbelievable, going from one extreme to the other like that. I still don't fully understand it — but that song saved my life. I'm not the sort to go all *touched by an angel*, but I've always believed Dad was there that day. He might not be around anymore, but he left a lot of love behind. And no power on Earth can take that away from me.

After the record finished, I put on another. And another. It was like I was experiencing music for the first time. I'd been numb for so long, but now, suddenly, I felt every song deeply. Every lyric. Every note. Their beauty and pain moved me to tears. Glorious tears. The kind of tears that remind you you're alive.

I completely lost track of time . . . until the doorbell rang.

Crap! The pizza guy!!

I bolted down the stairs but I was too late. The poor guy's face was green. The yellow Post-it hung limp between his trembling fingers. I still feel awful. He couldn't have been much older than I was.

'Damn kids and their pranks,' I said, doing my best to diffuse the situation.

'What?' he mumbled.

I chuckled unconvincingly. 'What does it say this time? Serial killer in the attic or body under the floorboards?'

'Dude! You have some messed up neighbours.'

'I know, right! Kids today — no boundaries. I blame TV.'

'Whatever,' he replied. 'You want the pizza or not?'

I paid for the pizza, adding a handsome tip for good measure. Then I devoured the entire thing in ten minutes flat. It was epic! My love of music wasn't the only thing that had returned. My appetite was back in action too. Afterwards, I grabbed a tub of chocolate chip ice-cream from the freezer, sprawled myself out on the couch and had a *SpongeBob SquarePants* marathon in honour of Saturday mornings with Dad.

If you'd told me that morning, I'd end the day laughing my head off in the company of copious amounts of junk food and a talking yellow sponge, I would've said you were nuts. But there I was. My life was by no means perfect. I knew I had a long road to recovery ahead. But I had my fight back. I wanted to live, and that was a start.

THE REAL WORK BEGAN a few days later when Mom got home. I told her everything. She was appalled, but also relieved. She's a mom, she'd known something was up.

'Oh honey, why would you ever wanna hurt yourself?' she asked, kissing my forehead as tears rolled down her cheeks.

'I felt like I was letting everyone down,' I said. 'I'm supposed to be the man of the house. I'm supposed to take care of you. That's what Dad would've wanted.'

'Theo, you aren't letting anyone down. And I can take care of myself. It's my job to take care of you.'

'I don't wanna hold you back.'

'You're not holding me back. Honey, after your dad

died, you were the only thing that kept me *holding on*.'

We were both full-on ugly crying by this stage. 'But I could've been buh-better,' I sobbed. 'Huh-helped you out more.'

'I could've handled things better too. We did the best we could with the hand we'd been dealt. And it was a fuckin' shitty hand.'

Mom never swore. We both giggled.

'Theo, the only thing you need to be is *happy*. That's all your father and I ever wanted. Stop putting all this pressure on yourself. The only shoes you need to fill are your own.'

'I might need some help with that,' I replied. 'I think I need to talk to someone.'

'Okay. I think that's a very good idea. We'll find someone. But in the meantime, you can always talk to me.'

Two days later, Mom arranged my first session with Hey-Jude. She's pretty incredible like that.

I REMEMBER THAT FIRST session like it was today. I was so nervous. My experience with Dr Green hadn't exactly imbued me with confidence. But this was different. This time, it was my choice. I entered Hey-Jude's office with an open mind.

The moment I walked through the door, any

comparisons to Dr Green were dispelled. There was nothing clinical or cold about Hey-Jude or his office. It felt homey. Mostly because it was his home — his office is on the second floor of his house. It's more of a study, really, filled with large bookcases, potted plants and colourful artwork.

Hey-Jude sat behind a polished mahogany desk that matched his bookcases. He was much younger than I'd expected. Mid-30s max. I'd been imagining some stuffy old professor type. No offence to stuffy old professors. But Hey-Jude is cool. He was wearing a suit, but it was slick — rich maroon and impeccably tailored. It complimented his ebony skin perfectly. Underneath he wore a silky cream shirt with no tie.

He extended his hand with a smile. 'Hi, Theodore, I'm Dr Johnson. But you can call me Jude.'

'Hey, Jude, you can call me Theo.'

He could see instantly that I was mesmerised by his library. 'You like to read, Theo?'

'Beats real life.'

'That's a shame. But I get what you mean. Life can be rough sometimes, and there's no greater escape than a good book.'

It was cool that we already had something in common right off the bat. He asked me to take a seat, and I sank into a comfy brown couch, looking at the rows of books behind him.

'You like Stephen King?' I asked. 'That's a pretty impressive collection.'

'Hell yeah! Who doesn't?' he said.

'My English teacher says horror writers are lowbrow. I tried explaining that King is more than a horror writer but he dismissed me just as quickly.'

'Your English teacher sounds a little bitter. You should give him a copy of *Rita Hayworth and Shawshank Redemption*.'

'Exactly.' I grinned.

'Do you have a favourite Stephen King novel?'

'I don't know if I can choose. I recently finished *Misery*, and I'm obsessed with Annie Wilkes. She may be the most terrifying villain he's ever created. What about you?'

'Can I choose two?' he asked.

'Sure.'

'It's a toss-up between *The Stand* and *The Shining*.'

'Nice,' I replied, before spotting the holy grail. 'Is that a UK first edition of *Carrie*?'

'Wow, you really are a fan. Nice spotting.'

'That must've cost a fortune.'

'I got a pretty good deal. But I'll admit, it's the most expensive book I own.'

I knew immediately we were going to get along just fine.

'So, what brings you here? I'm guessing you didn't come to talk about books.'

'I guess not. That'd be more fun, though.' I tugged at my sleeve, unsure where to begin.

'There's no pressure. We don't have to get straight into the heavy stuff. Why don't we start with how you're feeling today?'

'Today's okay, I guess. I was a little nervous about coming here. But it's not so bad.'

'I'm glad to hear that.' He smiled. 'Why were you nervous?'

'I'm not great at communicating.'

'You're doing pretty good so far.'

I could tell he meant it. And just like that, the words poured out of me. He listened attentively, nodding in encouragement and jotting down the occasional note. He must've realised the note-taking freaked me out, because he stopped and said, 'Anything I write down is for my eyes only. I just want to make sure I understand everything so we can figure this out together.'

I nodded. 'It's okay. I don't mind.'

I couldn't believe how quickly that first hour went by, or that I'd been the one who'd done most of the talking. Hey-Jude didn't say much. But the session really helped. He didn't look at me like I was crazy when I talked about the numbers or my suicide attempt. He made me feel normal.

I shook his hand vigorously before I left, genuinely thankful. But I still had one concern.

'I guess you're gonna recommend some type of medication?'

'Do you think that would help?' he asked.

'No. I'm not gonna hurt myself.'

'And I'm not gonna make you do anything you don't want to. Just promise you'll talk to me if you ever feel that way again, okay? I'm not saying I can wave a magic wand and make all your troubles disappear. You'll have real ups and downs. But talking is the first step. And that's what recovery is all about. Baby steps. You can reclaim your worth and reclaim your mind. One step at a time. Are you with me?'

I promised I was. And I meant it. I felt 10 pounds lighter when I left his study. I was even a bit disappointed that I had to wait another whole week for our next session.

CHAPTER EIGHT

HOW NOT TO DROWN — CHVRCHES

My sessions with Hey-Jude must be working, because I've finally asked Fly to meet up in person. Slots N' Slices just got three new arcade games, so I texted Fly to see if he wanted to check them out. He texted back immediately and was super chill. We're meeting there this weekend.

For anyone lucky enough to live outside of Fairview, Slots N' Slices is a retro arcade/diner. They make the best pizza and they have a decent range of vintage arcade games. The milkshakes are also pretty dope. It's one of the only cool places to hang in this town.

But now I'm freaking out. A couple of days ago it seemed a brilliant idea to meet up. I was proud of myself for finally nutting up and making it happen. There's just one minor problem . . . I'm nowhere near ready for it. What am I going to talk about? What will I wear? What's he gonna think when I can't make proper eye contact, let alone coherent conversation? It's not just about pizza and video games. Our entire friendship hangs in the balance. If this doesn't go well, he may not wanna talk to me anymore. I can't afford to lose the only friend I've got.

Maybe I should've left things as they were. Safely behind my trusty computer monitor where I'm not some awkward goon. In the Shadow Realm, I'm a dragon-slaying cyclops. Reality can't compete with that!

For any non-gamers out there, *The Shadow Realm of Lost Souls* is an MMORPG (massively multiplayer online role-playing game). Try saying that three times fast. Each player controls their own personalised avatar. You can customise your character however you want. The options are limitless. You can literally be *whoever* or *whatever* you want. It's totally F2P (free to play) but you can buy extra gear to pimp out your avatar. I prefer to win my gear through gameplay, completing challenges and earning crystals. Not because I'm cheap; it just feels more earned than using a credit card. It shows real skill and makes playing more worthwhile. But that's an ongoing debate within the gaming community.

Anyway, the core aim of the game is to protect the Realm from the Gloom. Or you can align yourself with the Gloom and try to destroy the Realm . . . if you wanna be a total dick! These players refer to themselves as the Legion of Gloom. Original, right?

Glooms are evil shadow monsters that feed on souls. When you defeat a Gloom, you set every soul it ever devoured free. The more souls you free, the more crystals you earn. And crystals equal currency, baby. They can be used to level up your character or buy new weapons and gear. It's awesome! New mini-challenges and maps are added weekly. You can also go there to hang out and talk to other players. I've met some odd ducks in the Realm. Once, I met an actual giant mutant duck.

Fly and I mostly spend our time annihilating the Legion. We've been hunting this one squad for over a month now. They started with 12 members, but we've blasted them down to five. Fly took three out last weekend alone.

Fly's avatar is sick! He's like Jeff Goldblum's Fly in the Cronenberg movie — but on steroids. He is basically this disgusting, muscled-up, fly/human hybrid. Fly's obsession with Jeff Goldblum is hardcore. He's seen all his movies — not just the biggies like *Jurassic Park* and *Independence Day*. He's ventured into deep-cut territory.

FairFlix is screening *Invasion of the Body Snatchers* this weekend. Fly asked if I wanted to go after Slots. I said yeah, because I've never seen it, but now I'm worried I'll screw things up and he'll change his mind.

Logic tells me to chill. But the chimpanzee doing cartwheels in my stomach overrides all logic. I know I should be excited, but I feel physically sick. The only other proper friend I've had is Ally — and look how that turned out.

I don't wanna lose Fly too. And I don't wanna see his number. It always changes everything. I can't invest in someone after I've seen the expiration date. I know I said I wanted to make a change — and I still do. Just not in this instance. My friendship with Fly is the one thing I want to stay the same.

Mom and Hey-Jude don't get our connection. They act like our friendship has no validity just because we've never met. They don't outright say it. But I can tell that's how they feel. Mom's always pushing me to ask him over for dinner or something equally cringe-worthy. As if that will make our friendship real. But it's *already* real to me. Which is why I'm hyperventilating.

The truth is, I've never felt whole. I've always felt like I have more missing parts than actual parts. But when I'm in the Realm I can be myself. Okay, I can also shoot a laser beam out of my eye and defeat monsters with my wise-cracking best friend. But in some ways, my life in the Realm is more real to me than my actual life.

Hey-Jude says I self-sabotage. He'd probably say that's what I'm doing right now. After all, it's not as if I like being alone. I pretend I'm a lone wolf by choice but most of the time I'm so lonely it kills me. I want to be a part of something. Part of the world like everyone else. I just don't know how. I'm not even sure it's the numbers' fault.

Maybe it's me. Maybe I'm the problem.

CHAPTER NINE

BLINDING LIGHTS — THE WEEKND

Neurotic outbursts are my specialty, and their timing is impeccable. I have one every time I make plans. I'm excited until the moment comes to follow through with said plans, then I freak out and cancel at the last minute. However, I didn't chicken out this time. Despite my urge to hide under the bedcovers and wait for the inevitable apocalypse to relieve me from all social obligations . . . I finally met Fly. Live and in the flesh.

Better yet, it wasn't a total disaster, even if the day didn't get off to the smoothest of starts.

I was rudely woken by my phone at 7 a.m.! What

kind of ungodly creature texts someone before noon on the weekend? There should be laws against such savagery.

We stil on 4 2nite? 6 @ Slots?

Reluctantly, I texted back. I pretended to be psyched. Before screaming into my pillow. Lying is so much easier via text.

Yeah, can't wait! See you there. 😊

Howl I no its u?

Spelling and grammar have never been Fly's forte. But I always get the gist. I told him I'd be sitting at one of the entrance booths and wearing my Jurassic Park T-shirt and sunglasses. He couldn't miss me.

Let's hope ur da only
dino luvin nerd there!

And that's exactly how I felt — like a nerd. It was pretty clear that Fly wasn't freaking out the way I was. This was just a typical Saturday for him. He probably met up with friends all the time and could afford to be nonchalant.

As for me, well, that little voice inside my head kept reminding me how inadequate I was. My hair looked goofy. My T-shirt was dorky. My jeans were too tight. And my shoes were stupid. None of these things looked any different from the way they usually did. Deep down, I knew this. But I was in an unshakable funk. After hours of relentless self-scrutiny and inventing implausible reasons to bail, I resigned myself to catastrophe. It was too late to cancel. He'd think I was a flake. Besides, if he wanted to reschedule, I'd have to go through the whole ordeal all over again. I decided the sooner I got this over with, the better.

I fidgeted my way through the day until it was time to leave. Then, I took a deep breath before making my way to Slots N' Slices. I slid my shades on and popped my earphones in to calm me down. I listened to The Weeknd on the way. Abel's flawless falsetto and synth-pop beats never fail to soothe my nerves.

Mom offered me a ride, but I opted to walk. I was ready to barf and needed the fresh air. Besides, the last thing I needed was Mom peering anxiously out the window when she dropped me off. She'd no doubt wish me luck and pat me on the back like a kid on his first day of school. No thanks. She was way too enthusiastic when I told her I was meeting Fly. You'd swear I'd got engaged. I had to cut her off before she congratulated me. I know she was only being supportive, but it made me feel even more pathetic than usual.

Slots N' Slices is my safe haven, as well as the town's biggest flex. The fact that it hasn't been refurbished since the '80s only adds to its charm. It's a cross between an arcade, a retro diner and a cheesy roller disco. No matter how much the world changes around it, Slots stays the same. It's stuck in its own little time warp. I guess you could say it's more than a place. It's also part of my history. Dad took Mom there on their first date. Plus, the tunes are epic! Best of the '80s all day, every day. And amid the commotion and flashing lights no one ever notices how awkward I am. Everyone has their head stuck in a game.

I arrived a few minutes early and slid into a booth facing the entrance. I puffed out my chest like a rooster, ensuring the Jurassic Park logo on my tee was on full display, and fiddled with the menu while I kept an eye on the door. Of course I'd forgotten to ask Fly what he'd be wearing, so I had no idea who I was looking for.

I've never felt more nauseous in all my life. Seconds felt like minutes. I memorised the entire menu front to back. To top it all off, I had to pee. Badly! I'd ordered a large Coke to stop the waitress from kicking me out of the booth. By the time I'd finished it, Fly was 10 minutes late and I was afraid to leave in case I lost the table or missed him arriving. I couldn't hold it much longer.

Then I began to worry I'd been stood up. I checked my phone to see if he'd texted to cancel, but there was nothing. I was literally getting up to leave when—

'Hey, loser! This seat taken?'

A dark-haired girl slid into the other side of the booth.

'It's all yours. I was just leaving,' I said.

'Leaving?' she growled. 'But I just got here!'

I was so startled, I broke my cardinal rule . . . I made eye contact.

I had no idea who this girl was. Or why she was gonna be part of my life for 71 days.

Until it hit me! She was Fly.

Mind. Blown.

'Hello, Earth to Theo!' the girl said.

'I have to pee,' I mumbled, before rushing to the restroom.

Not the smoothest of introductions, I'll admit. But my head was spinning. I did need to pee, but I also needed to re-evaluate everything I thought I knew about Fly from the safety of the restroom cubicle.

Did she lie to me? Or did I just assume she was a dude because of her username and avatar? We talked about guy stuff all the time, didn't we? Crap! That Jeff Goldblum obsession made a lot more sense. Jesus, what else had I misread? Was this a date???

I frantically emptied my bladder and washed my hands. I splashed some water on my face and fussed with my hair in the mirror before making my way back to our booth. Thankfully, she was still there, sipping on a Coke and twiddling the straw.

'Sorry,' I blurted. 'My bladder almost exploded. Didn't wanna lose the table, so I held it till you got here.'

She laughed. 'You looked like you were about to hurl. Am I really that hideous?'

'What? No! You're just not what I was expecting.'

She folded her arms, seemingly amused by my discomfort. 'How so?'

'Well, you're more attractive than your avatar. That's for sure.'

This was an understatement. She had a heart-shaped face with olive skin and full lips. Her black hair was chopped short, except on one side, where it hung below her chin. She wore a grey Nirvana tee under a red and black flannel shirt, with ripped skinny jeans and black Vans. I never thought of myself as someone who had a type. But, if I did, this was it.

She smiled. 'Is that so?'

'You're also a lot more . . . female.'

'Hold up!' She snorted. 'You thought I was a guy?'

'Maybe,' I replied, scratching my head like a monkey at the zoo.

'Why?' she howled.

'I dunno, your avatar's a guy.'

'My avatar is a mutant. How do you know it's a guy?'

'It has a bulge!'

'What?' She was still laughing. 'Why are you checking out my avatar's package?'

'I'm not. But it's hard to miss.'

'Is that why you brought me here? To check out my bulge?'

'No!' I could feel myself blushing. 'Your username is PrettyFly4aWhiteGuy98. How do you explain that?'

'Ugh, cringe!' She closed her eyes and slapped her forehead. 'I had an awful taste in music when I created my account. I thought it was funny. You know, 'cause I'm neither white nor a guy. Then I couldn't figure out how to change my username. So, I hoped people would figure I was being ironic or something.'

'But what about all those times we talked about how Buffy Summers is the perfect woman?'

'Dude, you don't need a penis to realise Sarah Michelle Gellar is the bomb!'

'So, you like girls?' I asked, trying to keep up.

'Guess so. Gender identity isn't really a deciding factor for me. I like who I like.'

'Cool,' I replied. And it was. I'd never met someone

this open. Fairview is a small town and not exactly hailed for its diversity.

'What about you?' she asked. 'Do you like girls, or are you only interested in mutated bulges?'

I'm not sure why, but I tensed up. No one had ever inquired about my sexuality.

'I like girls, I guess. But I haven't met enough people to rule anything out. I'm sort of a lone wolf. But I'm working on that with my therapist.'

I instantly regretted saying this. It was way too soon to bring my therapist into the conversation.

But she didn't seem shocked. 'Cool,' she said. 'My therapist says I need to set better boundaries. Apparently, I overshare.'

'I have the opposite problem.'

The tension eased temporarily — until I realised I was crushing on my best friend. I started assaulting the menu again.

'It's okay. I'm a girl, not an alien. I'm still the same person.'

'I know. I just feel like an idiot. There's so much I don't know about you.'

'That's easily fixed.' She grinned. 'Ask me anything. For one night only, I'm an open book. Just don't tell my therapist if I overshare.'

My mind went blank. I couldn't think of a single interesting question. Hyper-aware of how long I was taking to respond, I blurted out the first thing that came to mind.

'You have any pets?'

'Hard-hitting stuff.' She raised an eyebrow. 'No pets. I had a budgie once. But he died.'

'Oh, I'm sorry.'

'That's okay. Death was the only freedom that bird ever knew.'

We were silent for a moment, until she burst into a fit of giggles.

'That's poetic in a morbid sorta way,' I said.

'That's me,' she quipped.

I was done for. I fell faster than a drag queen performing a death drop during a lip-sync battle.

She must've caught me gawking at her, because she snapped her fingers. 'Come on, keep 'em coming. What else ya wanna know?'

'What was his name?' I spluttered.

'Who?'

'The budgie.'

'Let me get this straight . . . a girl says you can ask her anything and you wanna know the name of her dead budgie?'

I shrugged. 'I'm not very good at this game.'

'Relax. It's not a game. Just a conversation.'

'I'm not great at those either.'

Her expression softened. 'Blue.'

'Huh?'

'My budgie — his name was Blue.'

'Well, that spoils my next question.'

'How so?' she asked, taking a sip of her Coke.

'I was gonna ask what colour he was.'

She covered her mouth. But it was too late. Coke sprayed out between her fingers as she exploded with laughter. 'You really are something,' she said, grabbing a napkin to mop the table. 'There you go again, making assumptions.'

'Don't tell me he was yellow.'

'He was green.'

'You're not serious?'

'He looked so sad in his cage. I wanted to set him free. But my parents wouldn't let me. So I named him Blue.'

'That is tragic!'

'Like we established, that's sorta my vibe — poetic and morbid.'

'It's a winning combo.'

'I'm glad you think so,' she beamed. 'What about you, any dead pets?'

A look of dread shot across her face when I didn't answer.

'Oh god! Please tell me I didn't put my foot in my mouth. You haven't recently lost a beloved family dog or something?'

'Nope. You're good. No dead dogs — just a dead dad.'

'Right.' She laughed. 'Good one.'

I froze. I have no idea why I said that. Therapists and dead parents are not appropriate meet-cute topics.

'Wait, you are kidding?' she asked.

I contemplated lying, but that would have created a deeper hole for me to crawl out of.

'I'm sorry. I didn't mean to blurt it out like that.'

'Jeez, give a girl a heads-up. Now I feel like a jerk for laughing.'

'Don't, it's my fault. Like I said, I'm not great at this.'

'Is that why you're in therapy — 'cause of your dad?'

'That's part of it,' I replied gingerly.

'I'm sorry. We don't have to talk about it.'

I'd totally killed the mood. She looked as awkward as I felt.

'It's fine. Honestly. I brought it up. It was tactless.'

She reached over the table and playfully squeezed my shoulder. 'Well, if you ever need to talk, I'm not just an oversharer, I'm a pretty good listener too.'

'Thanks.' I smiled. 'But I'm good. It was a long time ago.'

'Still sucks!'

'Yeah, it does.'

She abruptly karate-chopped the air. 'So, we gonna kick some alien butt or what?'

'They have *Invasion of the Killer Pod Pigs 7*,' I said.

'Sweet! But first, isn't there one more question you should ask?'

I was stumped.

'Jeez, Theo, you learned my dead budgie's name before mine.'

I am so dense sometimes.

'It's Lily, by the way. Lily Sanchez. But just call me Lil. I still haven't forgiven my parents for naming me after a fucking flower.'

Lil Sanchez proceeded to kick my ass at every arcade game in Slots. She didn't even break a sweat. My palms were dripping trying to keep up. After her fourth consecutive win, she started doing this little victory dance, rubbing it in my face. She reminded me a lot of Ally.

Crap . . . I really do have a type.

We split a pizza when she was done obliterating me, and conversation flowed much more easily as the night progressed. Turns out I had nothing to worry about. Lil didn't rescind her movie invitation, after all. We watched *Invasion of the Body Snatchers* at FairFlix after Slots, and the movie was even better than she'd said.

We talked about *everything* and *nothing* on the way home, and I showed her how to change her username. R.I.P. Fly! She's now Lil-morbid-poet. It felt just like old times. Lil was right: she was still the same person I'd always known. But somehow everything was different.

I couldn't believe this awesome human had been right under my nose the whole time. What else had I been missing out on?

I'm still not sure if it was a date though. Maybe I'll ask Hey-Jude. He knows about these things.

There's just one problem . . . Lil's number.

What's gonna happen in 71 days? If we see each other every day, that's barely more than summer vacation.

At this point, I'd usually shut down and start building a wall between us. But I don't want to this time. I want to know everything about her, even if I don't see her again after she zeros out.

Does that make me a sucker for punishment?

CHAPTER TEN

DEAD OF NIGHT — ORVILLE PECK

I have a question . . . Why are there so many assholes in the world? I don't mean literal buttholes. Everyone's gotta poop. I'm talking about miserable people who crap on anyone who's not their carbon copy. What happened to celebrating our differences? Lately, it seems like the world has got more hateful. It's like the Facebook comment section has spilled into the real world.

I got an ugly dose of this before my most recent therapy session. The Fly/Lil situation had sent my head spinning, and I'd never been more eager to talk to Hey-Jude. I had so many questions and was excited to have new things to talk about. I even prepared notes.

But that all went out the window when I reached Hey-Jude's driveway. My train of thought was obliterated by three words that had been spray-painted in red on the side of his white Honda.

GOD HATES FAGGOTS

There was no doubt in my mind who was responsible. This had Barking Biddy written all over it! This was the second time she'd assaulted my faith in humanity in one week.

A couple of days earlier I'd spotted Hey-Jude at Fairview's FairPrice. He was shopping with his husband Elijah and their daughter Hope. I don't think they saw me. They were too preoccupied fending off Bridget Barker, the town's resident religious nut. It's hard to determine her age. She dresses like an elderly headmistress from a convent. Every inch of skin is covered with thick wool and tweed, no matter the temperature, but on closer inspection she's probably in her early 40s at most. The only embellishment she affords herself is a silver crucifix, which is always proudly on display. I don't know who coined the name Barking Biddy, but it's one shoe that sure as hell fits. Biddy is that delightful brand of Christian that skipped over all the 'love thy neighbour' and 'judge not lest ye be judged' passages of the Bible. Eternal damnation is more her jam. She'll take fire and brimstone over love and acceptance any day. I have no idea how bigots reconcile their hatred with their religion. I'm not religious, but even I can see they're missing the point.

I was about to pay for my extra-crunchy peanut butter at the checkout when I was subjected to Biddy's latest unsolicited sermon.

'That poor child,' Biddy howled, ensuring she was heard throughout the entire supermarket. 'She must be so confused.'

Hope is three years old and beyond adorable. Hey-Jude and Elijah adopted her last year.

'Excuse me,' Elijah retorted, 'the only thing confusing our child is your misplaced sympathy. You'd do best to worry about yourself, Ms Barker.'

'A girl needs a mother,' Biddy said, feigning concern.

'I can assure you, our daughter has everything she needs, including an abundance of strong, loving Black women to teach her how to handle ignorant old fools like you.'

Hey-Jude placed his hand on Elijah's shoulder, steering him away. 'Just ignore her, Eli. Don't waste your breath.'

'I'll pray for you, sweet girl,' Biddy called before launching into one of her *doom and gloom* Bible verses.

I watched as Hey-Jude and Elijah loaded groceries into their car. Elijah was visibly shaken. Hey-Jude smiled as he rubbed his husband's shoulders. But Biddy had clearly ruined their morning.

As for me, I wanted to march right up to Biddy and tell her to shove her prayers where the sun don't shine. Instead, I paid for my peanut butter and left.

I did nothing!

And I hated myself for it. What gave Biddy the right? Hey-Jude and Elijah are amazing parents. They have nothing but love in their hearts. I'd be way more concerned about a child growing up in a hate-filled home like Biddy's. I don't know how Hey-Jude kept his cool. I don't understand any of it. And it seemed like too much of a coincidence that Hey-Jude's car was vandalised a couple of days later.

'It's certainly no Banksy,' Hey-Jude said, looking up as I approached. He folded his arms while examining the affront on his car like you would a piece of art.

'How can you joke about this?' I asked.

'What's the alternative?' he said calmly. 'Cry. Get mad. Break something?'

'I dunno. It'd be a start.'

'Theo, we're two Black dudes raising a baby in a small town. If I reacted like that every time something like this happened, I'd be miserable for the rest of my life. Then who wins?'

'But you've gotta do something.'

'Don't worry, it's been reported. We're taking this

seriously. But without any eyewitnesses, the police don't have much to go on. They're questioning the neighbours as we speak. Hopefully, somebody can fill in a few blanks.'

'They should start by questioning Barking Biddy.'

Hey-Jude laughed as if I'd suggested Dennis the Menace was the culprit. 'What makes you think Ms Barker had something to do with this?'

'Are you kidding? After that scene she made at FairPrice — how can you *not*?'

'Ah, you caught that little show?'

'I'm pretty sure the whole store caught it.'

Hey-Jude nodded. 'That's unfortunate. But can you honestly picture Ms Barker running around in the middle of the night with a can of spray paint?'

'No, but that doesn't mean she's not responsible. She's getting Fairview's nutjobs all riled up again.'

'Maybe you've got a point, Sherlock.' Hey-Jude patted me on the back and nudged me towards his front door. 'But how about we let the police take care of it. I'm sure we've got more interesting things to discuss than my new paint job.'

I dropped the subject and headed inside. But my issues suddenly felt trivial.

'So, what's going on, besides my unrepentant homosexuality?' Hey-Jude asked.

I couldn't help but laugh. I swear, Hey-Jude could disarm a bomb with those pearly whites. I sank into his comfy leather couch and relaxed. 'How do you know if someone's flirting with you?'

'Huh?' he replied.

I gave him a complete rundown of my evening with Lil. He did his best to explain the complexities of flirting. Unfortunately, I'm now more confused than ever. Apparently, if someone picks on you a lot, they might have a crush on you or they may just hate your guts. There's also body language, chemistry and a plethora of other factors to consider. Sometimes it's super-obvious when someone likes you, and other times it's more subtle. It all depends on the person. You've got to somehow decipher how they feel by trusting your intuition and reading social cues. Neither of which is my strong suit. The whole thing is a total mindfuck.

However, Hey-Jude did clear one thing up. He said that if neither of us specified that it was a date, then it was safer to assume it wasn't. He cleverly deduced that Fly being Lil, and Lil being female, doesn't automatically change the nature of our relationship. If we've always been friends, then we're probably still just friends.

I felt like a dummy. But I still think there was some flirting at play. So I'm gonna take Hey-Jude's advice and trust my intuition and start working harder at reading those social cues.

Luckily, I got some more practice . . . My pocket buzzed as soon as I left his house.

> Rents are out! Wanna come
> ovr and kik sum Gloomer ass?

Hell yeah, I did!

But I did a double take when I got to Lil's house. It looked different in daylight, way bigger than how it had seemed when I walked her home a few nights earlier. It must be the swankiest place in Fairview. I tucked my shirt into my jeans and combed back my wildly uncooperative hair before I pressed the buzzer.

Lil looked a little spooked when she answered the door. 'Were you lurking outside my house or something?'

'What? No . . . why?'

'How'd you get here so fast? I literally just texted you.'

'Oh, I was at Hey-Jude's. He lives nearby.'

'Hey-Jude?' She looked more confused than relieved.

'He's my therapist.'

Note to self: you don't have to bring your therapist into every conversation.

'Okay, creeper.' Lil moved aside to let me in. 'You can explain why your therapist's name is Hey-Jude while I pulverise the Gloomer nest I've been tracking for the past two hours.'

Lil's pad was even more swish on the inside. It was like walking inside one of those fancy homeware catalogues. I never knew there were so many different shades of beige. It was hard to believe people lived in this house. I felt like I needed to be disinfected before touching anything. Until we reached the basement . . .

'Welcome to my lair,' Lil said. 'My respite from the dull conformism that's infested the rest of the house.'

I could finally picture Lil living in this otherwise spotless McMansion. The basement was an amalgam of cables and paintbrushes. It was as messy and beautiful as Lil. Not a hint of beige in sight. Every inch of wall space was filled with the most incredible artwork. One half of the room was packed with art supplies and half-finished sculptures, the other had the sweetest gaming set-up I've ever seen. Complete with a comfy reclining sofa, a huge flat-screen TV, a refrigerator stocked with soda and a coffee table piled high with snacks. Be still my beating heart.

My mouth was hanging open like I'd just discovered the pirate ship in *The Goonies*. 'This is awesome!' I blurted as my eyes gravitated back to the detailed sketches and colourful paintings that plastered the walls, all of them with the same signature at the bottom. Mythical creatures and exotic landscapes brought the room to life. It was like walking into a fantasy world. I suddenly realised I'd just stepped inside Lil's brain.

'Did you do all of these?'

'It's no big deal. Just a hobby.'

'Video games are a hobby,' I replied. 'These are incredible.'

'They don't suck. It's therapeutic. I'm not trying to make a career out of it or anything.'

'Why not? You could make a lot of money.'

'Not according to my dad.'

'No offence to your dad, but I strongly disagree.'

'Thanks. But he's not a jerk or anything. He's just trying to look out for me. There are tons of artists way more talented than me barely making ends meet.'

'There's also a ton with half your talent raking in the dough.'

She shrugged. 'I was gonna apply to art school, but my parents convinced me to take a business course at Fairview Tech in September instead.'

'You sound thrilled,' I teased.

'We fought about it for a while. But they're probably right. I can't expect my folks to feed and clothe me forever. I've gotta be realistic. Besides, it's not so bad. Maybe I can use what I learn to market my art.'

'I guess that's smart. But you should apply to the art school too.'

'Too late. Admissions closed last week.' She nudged my shoulder. 'Now, are we gonna kick some Gloomer ass or braid each other's hair?'

'You think I could pull off a braid?'

She laughed, and I wondered whether we were flirting.

'I still think you should apply,' I said. 'I'm sure they'd make an exception if they saw these.'

'It's a very prestigious school. They don't make exceptions. But thanks, you're sweet.'

I could see she was pleased, but I didn't want to overstep. 'I like this song playing. Who is it?' I asked, picking up one of the controllers.

'It's Orville Peck. I'm obsessed.'

'Oh, of course. I love Orville.'

'You have no idea who he is, do you?'

'Not a clue.' I giggled. 'My music taste is a little dated.'

'Dated is cool too. But I'll make you a mixtape.'

'Old-school. I like it. No one's ever made me a mixtape.'

'Well, prepare to have your mind blown. Orville is a psychedelic dreamboat in a cowboy hat. He's like Zorro, Dolly Parton and Elvis all rolled up into one.'

'Sounds epic.'

'Oh, he is!'

I really did love the song. I'd never heard anything like it. It was retro and contemporary at the same time.

I told Lil about what happened to Hey-Jude's car while we played video games. Turns out she'd already heard. News travels fast in Fairview. She agreed that Biddy must have played her part. Lil's parents made her go to church every Sunday. She'd seen Biddy regularly handing out pamphlets opposing gay marriage after the service. Biddy might not have paint on her hands, but this was happening because of her fearmongering.

'I knew it!' I felt validated and outraged simultaneously. 'She shouldn't be allowed to get away with this!'

'I have an idea,' Lil replied. 'Let's hit pause on the game for today. Biddy's not the only activist in town.' She threw a hoodie over her head and grabbed a backpack from under the coffee table. 'Are you coming or what?'

'Where?'

She marched on like a woman on a mission while I struggled to keep up. It was already dark out, and I had no idea where we were going. But my Spidey sense was tingling. It went into full alert when we stopped outside Biddy's house.

'What are we doing here?' I asked.

'Shhhhh!' Lil hissed, before opening her bag and taking out a can of spray paint.

'This is a bad idea. Let's go home,' I said.

'You were the one who said she shouldn't get away with it.'

'I know, but Hey-Jude's right. We should let the cops take care of this.'

She rolled her eyes. 'You really think the cops can

do anything? They can't pin this on Biddy. But that doesn't mean she's not responsible.'

'Okay, fine. But hurry, the lights are on inside.'

There was no changing her mind, and I'd be lying if I said Biddy didn't deserve it. But I couldn't get Hey-Jude's voice out of my head. He'd never approve.

'Keep an eye out,' Lil whispered.

I watched the house carefully as Lil went to town on Biddy's car. The hiss of spray paint echoed in the dead of the night. She stepped aside when she was done, proudly unveiling her latest masterpiece.

GOD HATES BIGOTS!

The words popped in neon pink. Two wrongs may not make a right, but it felt like justice.

We only had a few seconds to admire Lil's handiwork before the front door swung open. We scurried off like mice after spotting a buzzard.

'I'M CALLING THE COPS!' Biddy yelled. 'YOU HOODLUMS!'

We ran until our lungs gave out. We made it all the way to the town park and collapsed on the grass.

'That was awesome,' Lil howled.

'You're insane,' I panted. 'But in a good way.'

'All the best people are a little insane.'

'Agreed. But could you give me a heads-up next time

you decide to make me an accomplice in one of your felonious forays?'

'Felonious forays? Who are you?'

'I'm just a boy. Standing in front of a girl. Asking her not to give him cardiac arrest.'

'Did you just quote *Notting Hill*?'

'What? Guys watch rom coms too.'

She squinted like she was trying to solve a puzzle. 'You're a unique individual, Theodore Brown.'

'Is that bad?' I asked.

'No. It's sort of beautiful.' She kissed me on the forehead, winked, then ran off. 'See you tomorrow, weirdo.'

'Tomorrow?' I shouted after her.

'Yeah. Tag, you're it! You can choose our next *felonious foray*.'

Okay, I'm no expert. But if that wasn't flirting . . . I give up!

I usually find winking creepy. It's generally reserved for douchey bros in bars hitting on girls who are too young for them. But when Lil winked at me, my insides went berserk. Forget butterflies, I had pterodactyls flapping around my tummy.

She used the word beautiful . . . in relation to *me*. Plus . . . she *kissed* me!

Okay, it was on the forehead. But a kiss is a kiss.

There's something between us. I know it. When

we're together, my head feels like it could fly right off my shoulders and vanish into the clouds like a balloon. But I also feel like I've swallowed a bowling ball. I feel light and heavy at the same time. This dizzying dichotomy throws me completely off balance.

I guess that's why they call it *falling* in love, because I feel like I'm about to faceplant. And the only thing I can think about is when I'm going to see her again.

I played 'Dead of Night' repeatedly when I got home, deciphering its lyrics carefully. The song hit differently when I listened to it alone. I discovered it was all about a love that didn't last. Go figure! But there's hope in its melancholy. It sounds like Orville gained more than he lost from the relationship in the song. I couldn't help but wonder if I had more to gain or lose over the next 70 days with Lil.

CHAPTER ELEVEN

ANTI-HERO — TAYLOR SWIFT

I died when I spotted the cops in Hey-Jude's driveway this morning!

Okay, I'm being hyperbolic with the whole dying thing. But I stood frozen at the far end of the street like an ornate statue with a guilty conscience. The cops were obviously there because of Lil's impromptu art demonstration.

Hey-Jude scratched his head as an officer scribbled in her notebook. He'd clearly spotted me gawking, because he lingered in the front doorway after the cops drove off. I tried to act cool as I crossed the street. *Stay calm. He can't possibly know you have anything to do with this. There's no way Biddy could've seen us.*

'Theodore Brown, you wouldn't know anything about Bridget Barker's car being vandalised last night, would you?' he called.

'Who, me? Of course not! Maybe it was the same person who did a number on yours!'

I was surprised at how swiftly I lied. Hey-Jude and I had made a deal to always be honest with one another. I never imagined I'd break that promise with such ease.

'That seems unlikely,' he replied, 'given the contrasting nature of the two messages.'

'Really? What did hers say?' I asked.

Hey-Jude's eyes narrowed. 'You sure you need me to answer that? Yesterday you went off about how Bridget Barker ought to get what's coming to her, and her car was graffitied that very same night . . . What a coincidence.'

'I'd call it karma. But other than that, I'm in the dark. I was with Lil all evening. Besides, Barking Biddy has made her fair share of enemies. It could've been anyone.'

'I'm sorry, Theo, you're right. You've got more sense than that. But if you hear anything about our mysterious vigilante—'

'You'll be the first to know,' I said.

I felt like a snake. But I couldn't squeal on Lil.

'So, how'd things go with Miss Sanchez?' Hey-Jude's posture immediately softened.

'That's sort of why I'm here. I know we don't have an appointment today but I could really use your advice.'

'Sure, I have a few minutes to spare.'

I followed Hey-Jude into his sleek kitchen. It was weird talking outside of his study. It felt more like chilling with a friend.

'You want something to drink?' he asked.

'Sure, I'll have a beer.'

Hey-Jude chuckled as he set two tall glasses on the counter before grabbing a jug of freshly squeezed juice from the fridge. 'You like mango?'

I nodded as he filled the glasses to the top. 'The cops don't think you had anything to do with Biddy's car?' I asked.

'No, but Ms Barker seems to. She told the police she saw two Black teenagers fleeing the scene.'

What the actual fuck? Not only is Biddy a homophobic piece of shit but she's also a frigging racist!

'She's such a liar!' I growled.

Hey-Jude tilted his head. 'How do you know she's lying?'

'Because it's obviously bullshit! She's just trying to push her hateful agenda.'

'You're probably right.' He sighed. 'Unfortunately,

there will always be those who believe the Bridget Barkers of the world.'

'Remind me again how you can stand that?'

Hey-Jude shrugged. 'Everyone has a thing.'

I had to stop myself from laughing. 'Say what now?'

'Let me rephrase that.' He grinned. 'Everyone has struggles. Everyone is fighting their own private battle. For you, it's the numbers. For me, it's homophobia and racism. For Ms Barker, it's probably something much darker. That kind of hate can only come from deep self-loathing and fear.'

'That doesn't explain how you stop yourself from screaming. I'd want to punch a hole in the world.'

Hey-Jude opened his wallet and took out a photo of his family wearing Halloween costumes and pulling funny faces. Hey-Jude was dressed as the Tin Man, Elijah was the Cowardly Lion and Hope was the cutest little Dorothy I've ever seen. 'I look to them,' he said proudly. 'I look at my beautiful family and I'm filled with joy. It's about gratitude. Plain and simple. My family's what matters. I care what *they* think — not some ignorant fool like Bridget Barker.'

'But don't you get tired of people like her?'

'Sometimes. And on those days I practise gratitude the hardest. We can't choose how the world treats us, Theo. But we can choose how we react. And I choose love. Every time.'

I started to understand why Hey-Jude was always smiling. Barking Biddy still infuriates me. But I'm not going to let her poison my heart too.

'Now, tell me all about your girl troubles.'

I cringed. 'That seems sort of superficial now.'

'Not at all.' Hey-Jude waved dismissively. 'Comparative suffering is a fruitless game. You're young, this is exactly the type of thing you're supposed to be stressing about. I think it's great that you're finally putting yourself out there.'

It sounded trivial, but I described my evening with Lil in pedantic detail. I omitted our little arts-and-crime spree, obviously. But I told him about the kiss, and he agreed that flirting was highly probable. But he advised I play it cool for now.

'I have no idea where to take her this evening,' I groaned. 'It's not a date. But it's not 100 percent not a date either. Am I making any sense?'

Hey-Jude laughed. 'Just relax. Think of it as a pre-date.'

'What the hell do you do on a pre-date?'

'You get to know each other better. You need to determine if there's more than friendship at play, and whether you're compatible for more than that.'

'So . . . dinner and a movie?' I threw my head back and sighed. 'No, that's too datey!'

'You mentioned she showed an interest in your record collection. Why don't you invite her over? Play some smooth tunes . . . A little Marvin Gaye can work wonders.'

'That's not a bad idea,' I admitted. 'But don't you think I should plan something *bigger*?'

'It's early days. There'll be time for *bigger* later.' He quickly looked at his watch. 'Speaking of later, I better get a move on. Are we all good, my man?'

'Yeah, we're better than good. And for the record, I think Hope is the luckiest kid in Fairview to have you and Elijah for parents.'

Hey-Jude's face lit up. 'Thanks, bud. Now go use some of that smooth talk on Lily Sanchez.' He gave me a supportive pat on the back before releasing me into the wild.

I wish everyone had a Hey-Jude in their lives. The world would be a much kinder place. His advice was exactly what I needed. All I had to do was relax and invite Lil over. Easy.

I ran home and frantically tidied my pigsty of a room. I removed all my dirty laundry and rearranged my books and furniture in every possible combination. I borrowed one of Mom's scented candles but worried that might seem too try-hard . . . Luckily, I remembered to put Henry in the closet. Henry the herbivore is my stuffed dinosaur. I've had him since I was four. He's a Brachiosaurus, and he usually lives on my bed. But Lil doesn't need to know this.

My room feels kind of basic compared to Lil's. But I have an impressive library and record collection, and I'm hoping she'll find those interesting.

All that's left to do is: *Breathe. Keep it simple. Exhale.*

CHAPTER TWELVE

BOYS DON'T CRY — THE CURE

I've officially entered my douchebag era. From here on out, you can call me Theodore Jackass-Brown.

I invited a sweet, intelligent, funny girl over to my house, and what did I do? I acted like a jerk, let my fragile male ego take the wheel, and drove her away!

Who could blame her if she never wanted to see me again? But unfortunately, Lil will have to endure my company for another 68 days. Because the numbers don't lie. Hopefully, she won't hate my guts for the entire duration.

Lil arrived around 6.30 p.m. She got all shy and overly polite when I introduced her to my mom. I'd never seen that side of her. She even managed to make awkward look cute.

Mom was her excessively enthusiastic self. You'd swear I'd sprouted wings and a unicorn horn when I first told her a girl was coming over.

'Should I make snacks? I should make snacks. Does she like hummus? No. I should go. I should leave, right? Give you guys some space?'

'You don't have to leave, Mom. It's not a big deal,' I said before her head exploded.

In Mom's defence, she was chill when Lil arrived. Apart from some overzealous handshaking, she was cool as a cucumber and left us alone once the obligatory parental niceties were over. I took Lil to my newly organised room and pretended it was always this neat and tidy. 'Just Like Heaven' by The Cure was casually spinning on the record player as we entered. It's not like I spent an hour deciding which record to play before she arrived or anything. Okay, it was more like two hours. Did I mention I'm a chronic overthinker?

'I like your digs. It's tidy for a guy's room,' Lil said, nervously brushing a lock of dark hair from her face and tucking it behind her ear. 'Not that I've been in many guys' rooms before.' She blushed before quickly changing the subject. 'Do I smell pumpkin spice?'

'It's the candle. I can blow it out if you don't like it?'

Lil raised her hand in protest. 'No. It's nice. I love pumpkin.'

'Me too. It's so versatile. You've got roast pumpkin. Pumpkin pie. Pumpkin spice lattes . . . and it makes a cool Halloween decoration.'

Sweet Jesus, someone stop me, I thought.

Lil cut the tension with her infectious laugh. I don't know why it was so awkward. It wasn't weird when we hung out at her house. I guess that was different. That was in the basement. Bedrooms make things weird.

'I love The Cure,' she said.

Thank you, Robert Smith, you never fail me.

'I know, right? They're the best.'

I realised I'd been standing gawkily in the middle of the room the entire time. I felt like I had more limbs than I knew what to do with. I quickly grabbed the album cover and plonked myself on the floor next to my record chest. My body relaxed almost immediately.

Lil sat down next to me. '"Boys Don't Cry" is my favourite.'

'Yeah, it's one of mine, too.'

She started sifting through my record collection. 'Cool treasure chest.'

'Storage is key for vinyl enthusiasts. You've gotta keep them vertical so they don't warp.'

'You're such a nerd,' she said.

I knew she was only joking. But I felt burned.

Records are delicate. My dad drilled that into me. He showed me how to handle them. How to play them. How to clean them. And how to store them. It's all part of the ritual. It was our thing. It's become sort of sacred to me. 'Gently take the record out,' Dad would say. 'Only hold it by the edges and the label. We don't wanna muddy the grooves with fingerprints. You've got to be gentle if you want them to keep singing sweetly.'

'I love this one!' Lil squealed, pulling Fleetwood Mac's *Mirage* from the record chest. 'When I first discovered this, I listened to nothing but "Gypsy" for a week straight.' She yanked the record out of its sleeve. My stomach twisted as her fingers met the surface of the vinyl.

Without thinking, I snapped it from her. Then I quickly grabbed some liquid record cleaner from my dresser and wiped it gently. I wasn't trying to be a dick. It was a visceral reaction.

Lil's face was aghast. 'My hands are clean. I wasn't gonna break it or anything.'

'You can't just grab them like that. Hands are oily. Oil attracts dust. It diminishes the sound quality.' I regretted the words the moment they left my mouth. Again I was acting on pure instinct. My words hung in the air like a bad fart.

Lil stared at me like I was a toddler throwing a

tantrum in a supermarket. 'Noted. I'll keep my oily paws to myself in future.'

'I'm sorry. I didn't mean to go all fun-police on you. It's just . . . these records belonged to my dad.'

Her expression softened. 'I'm sorry, I wasn't trying to damage it or anything.'

'You don't need to apologise. It's my bad. I over-reacted.'

'You weren't one of those kids who invited people over to play but wouldn't let anyone touch your toys, were you?'

'What? No! I fucking hate those kids.'

She laughed. 'Good, me too.'

I finished cleaning the record and played 'Gypsy' for her. She swayed to the music, and social equilibrium was restored. She glided over to my bookcase and skimmed the spines with her fingertips. 'Is it okay to touch the books?'

'Absolutely, I highly encourage book touching.' I felt blood rush to my cheeks. 'Sorry, that sounded weirdly sexual.'

'How many books do you own?' she asked.

I shrugged. 'I dunno, hundreds, I guess.'

'Never knew you were such a Poindexter.'

'I'm not. I just like to escape. That's also why I like video games. But books are even better. You can go anywhere. Be anyone. Get lost for hours. Sometimes days. I hope to write my own one day. But my professor says I need to get a life first — see the world and get jaded or some shit.'

'I might have to agree with him.'

She was only messing with me. But this was the third dig in a row, and it made me defensive.

'The best art usually derives from some kind of pain,' she added.

'Trust me, I know pain. Intimately. We're long-time besties. Just because I don't go around vandalising other people's property doesn't mean I haven't lived.'

'Ouch!' Lil placed her hand on her chest. 'I didn't mean to touch a nerve.'

'You didn't,' I replied, even though she totally had. 'I'm just saying you don't need to be reckless or self-destructive to create great art.'

'You didn't seem to mind my *recklessness* last night. I thought I was "insane in a good way".'

'Well, now that I've had time to process it, I think it was dumb. You could've got Hey-Jude in trouble.'

'Chill out. No one is gonna suspect your therapist of vandalism,' she sneered.

'Yeah, tell that to Hey-Jude. He spent the morning with the cops.'

'Shit! Are you serious? I didn't think—'

I interrupted before she could finish. 'That's just it. You didn't think. Barking Biddy told the cops she saw two Black teens fleeing the scene. What if some innocent kids take the fall?'

'I wouldn't let that happen.' Lil stood up and marched to the door. 'Because unlike you, I'm not a total jerk.'

I tried to apologise. But she wasn't interested. And I didn't blame her. It was cruel of me to drop that on her out of the blue. I knew she'd never let anyone take the fall for her.

'I made this for you,' Lil said, dropping something on my bed. 'I hope my oily fingers haven't diminished the sound quality.' Then she stormed off.

It was the mix CD she'd promised. I sat on the edge of the bed and read the handwritten tracklist on the cover. She'd scrawled Welcome to the 21st Century on the disc. It was filled with artists I'd never heard of, aside from Orville Peck. I felt like a monster. This was the sweetest thing anyone had ever done for me.

So much for boys don't cry. I was a total mess after the first couple of songs.

Then Mom poked her head in the door. Her timing was impeccable, as always. 'You okay, honey?'

'I'm fine. I just wanna be alone,' I sobbed.

'Your friend left in a hurry.'

'I don't wanna talk about it.'

'How about I bring you a sandwich. I made some in case you two got hungry.'

I shoved my face into my pillow and screamed. ‘I DON’T WANT A SANDWICH! JUST LEAVE!’

‘Suit yourself. But you can’t take your issues out on everyone else. Eventually, you’re going to have to grow up, Theodore.’

I was two for two. I’d managed to offend the two most important women in my life within minutes of each other. Nice one.

CHAPTER THIRTEEN

IF I COULD TURN BACK TIME — CHER

After two full days of solid wallowing, I've decided enough is enough. The time for sulking has passed. I've adequately honed my brooding skills and acquired a cute new bed sore. His name is Bumpy and, to be honest, he's a pain in the ass. Pun intended.

I'm now a man of action and ready to make amends.

Winning Mom over was easy. I got up extra-early and made a sneaky trip to the grocery store for all the ingredients to make her breakfast of choice: smashed avocado and poached eggs on sourdough. I even got the funky-smelling vinaigrette she likes. I'm officially her can-do-no-wrong golden boy again. And it only cost me $16.50. Bargain!

After I'd served it up, I took a seat at the table and we tucked in. It was no French toast. I'll take syrupy goodness over sour vinaigrette any day. But Mom loved it and that's what mattered. It wasn't as pretty as the version they make at her favourite brunch place, but it was a hell of a lot cheaper.

When she'd finished, Mom held her coffee mug snug in both hands and said, 'You wanna talk about it?'

She didn't even have to say Lil's name. I knew what she meant.

'No . . . Yes . . . I don't know.'

'That bad, huh?'

'Bad is forgetting to wear deodorant or realising you're in dire need of a breath mint. Yesterday was cataclysmic!'

'You really like her.'

This wasn't a question. She just knew it to be true the way moms often do.

'Yeah, but I'm hopeless at this stuff.'

'What stuff?'

'People. Girls. Dating . . . life! I suck at all of it. I wish I was more like Dad.'

Mom laughed so suddenly, I spluttered coffee down my chin.

'You think your father was always good at that stuff?'

'Well, yeah. Wasn't he?'

'No! He was awkward as hell on our first few dates. He barely said two words. Meanwhile, I babbled profusely to compensate. It was painful.' She chuckled. 'I thought he'd never want to hear another word from me again. He was so shy when he was younger. But sweet. Always sweet.'

She squeezed her ringless wedding finger and blushed. She does this a lot when she talks about Dad. I've always wondered if she knows she's doing it. But I've never asked.

'I can't imagine Dad being shy.'

'It was a long time ago. The two of you are more alike than you realise.'

'But you guys were always so at ease around each other. How did you get past the awkwardness?'

Mom sat her coffee on the table and thought carefully. 'Time,' she replied at last, then paused again. 'There's no cheat. You just keep talking, and each time you do, it gets a little easier. Everyone has insecurities. We try so hard to cover them up when we first meet someone. But there's no point in hiding who you are. If you really like this girl, show her *all* of you. Not just the shiny parts. Sure, she'll realise you're not perfect. But that's okay. Because trust me, she's not either. That's the whole point — that's what love is . . . it's embracing the whole picture. Warts and all.

It's about finding that one person that's imperfectly perfect for you.'

As usual, Mom was right. I've just gotta be my nerdy, awkward self. That's who I've always been with Lil. I didn't worry about this stuff before we met in person. But after the countless hours we've spent gaming and chatting online, she knows what a massive geek I am. Because she's one too. And that's okay. No — it's better than okay, it's great. Or at least it would be if I could convince her to give me another chance.

I thanked Mom and gave her a big hug. I even offered to do the dishes. But she told me to go sort things out with Lil. Easier said than done, though luckily I'd had one of those lightbulb moments during Mom's motivational speech.

I went to my room and grabbed my favourite book from the shelf. I sat at my desk and carefully inscribed it. Then I sprinted to Lil's house. I placed the book on her doorstep, rang the doorbell, ran back and ducked behind a car across the street, and waited for the door to open. Thankfully, it was Lil who came out. As she looked around to see who had called, I sent her a link to Cher's 'If I Could Turn Back Time' music video. She took her phone out of her pocket and listened as the song began to play. This earned me half a smile. She scanned the perimeter again before spotting the book. I sent her a text message as she picked it up.

Open Me 😊

She opened the book.

Dear Lil,

Unfortunately, I can't turn back time. All I can do is apologise. I was an insecure turd and I'm unworthy of your friendship. But I'm hoping you'll hang with me anyway. Because you're the coolest person I know, and I can't take down the Legion of Gloom without you. The last thing I wanted to do was hurt your feelings. If you forgive me, I promise it will never happen again.

PS I love the mix CD. I've been listening to it non-stop.

PPS I wanted to share something with you in return. Timothy's Terrible Time Machine is my Favourite Book. I've spent a lot of time wishing I had a time machine of my own these past couple days. But I'm hoping I can make things right without one.

Love,

Theodore (Jackass) Brown

She snapped the book shut, narrowed her eyes and scoured the neighbourhood one last time before heading back inside.

I waited anxiously for my phone to ping as I walked home. But there was nothing. I couldn't be sure she'd read the whole message, but honestly I was hoping my words were going to spark more of a reaction.

Hours went by. And nada. Nothing. Radio silence.

I tried to distract myself with books and TV. But it was useless. I wanted to call her but kept second-guessing her reaction. Now I thought about it, I couldn't decide whether my make-up attempts were sweet or plain creepy?

I decided the only way to take my mind off things was to exterminate some Gloomers.

After about an hour of wandering the Realm, Lil's avatar approached me. That monstrous fly/human hybrid never looked more beautiful. Then Lil sent me a text.

Thers a nest of 6 Gloomers in the Forbidden Forest. You got enuf ammo?

Locked and loaded!

That Gloomer nest never stood a chance. Lil took out three of them in under two minutes. I wiped out another two, and we spent an hour hunting the last, the biggest and ugliest of the pack. He got his rocks off by terrorising wood nymphs. The sprite and nymph community have been hit hard in the Realm recently. Eventually, we cornered the sadist and finished the job together. As a reward, the nymphs awarded us unlimited safe passage through the Forbidden Forest. Lil and I didn't talk about the argument. Or my weird attempt at an apology. We just gamed. Like old times. It was uncomplicated and easy. I played it cool but felt like I'd won the lottery.

CHAPTER FOURTEEN

BIRDS OF A FEATHER — BILLIE EILISH

Isn't life grand? I'm currently spinning around in a picturesque alpine meadow, singing at the top of my lungs. Okay, that's a lie. I'm spinning around in my dank bedroom. But I finally understand what Julie Andrews was singing about on those damn hills. It's taken 19 years. But I get it. And all it took was a kiss. No kidding. Lil kissed me. Me! Theodore Brown. And not on the cheek. For real. So, I'll be damned if I don't spin until I barf.

The day in question started out like any other. Eggs for breakfast, therapy for lunch. I told Hey-Jude all about my latest screw-up. But he was impressed I managed to dig my way out of that hole without him.

'I couldn't have done it without Mom,' I said.

'You asked for advice when you needed it. That's a big step forward,' he replied.

'I guess. But I also created the whole mess in the first place. So really, it's more like one step back, one step forward. Which puts me where I've always been.'

Hey-Jude shook his head. 'So, you messed up. Welcome to the human race. You owned your mistakes and made amends. Give yourself credit. Sometimes conflict is necessary for growth.'

'Thanks, Dr Phil.'

Hey-Jude brushed some imaginary dust off his shoulder. 'Please, Dr Phil ain't got shit on me.'

We both laughed. It was uncharacteristic of Hey-Jude to swear.

'You must really like this girl,' he added, echoing Mom's words.

'I do,' I groaned. 'But it doesn't matter how I feel.'

'Of course it matters.'

My eyes wandered to the painting on the wall behind Hey-Jude's desk. I usually find landscapes boring, but I've always liked this one with its geometric designs and the vibrancy of the trees. I got lost in it for a moment. Its warm colours were more comforting than the cold truth.

Hey-Jude clicked his fingers to regain my attention.

'Theo, what makes you think your feelings don't matter?'

'Because I've seen her number,' I snapped, crashing back to reality.

'I see.' Hey-Jude nodded. 'How long do you have?'

I buried my face in my hands. 'Until the end of summer if we keep seeing each other this frequently.'

'What happens after summer?' he asked.

'I dunno. Like I've said, all I get is the number. If I had a *how* or a *why*, maybe I could change things. But I don't.'

Hey-Jude took a moment to reply. 'The way I see it,' he said at last, 'you've got two choices.'

'Enlighten me.'

'Option one — you spend the summer sulking, and you both have a miserable time.'

'Please tell me option two is less depressing.'

'Option two is infinitely less depressing.' He paused for dramatic effect.

'Well, don't leave me hanging! What is it?'

'You stay present. Live in the moment, like we've been discussing. Make the most of each day you've got, instead of worrying about the ones you don't. Who knows, maybe you'll have such a great summer together, the number will change.'

'Nothing changes the number! This isn't some self-fulfilling prophecy crap. I can't change the outcome with positive thinking.'

Hey-Jude is the only person I've been totally honest with. The idea that he'd been humouring me this whole time was triggering to say the least.

'Maybe you're right,' Hey-Jude replied gently. 'But have you ever given it a real shot?'

If I'm honest, I probably hadn't. But how could I deny what's literally staring me in the face?

'Are we honestly going back to this cognitive therapy bullshit? I thought we'd moved beyond this.'

'I'm just saying that changing the narrative might help. The stories we tell ourselves are powerful. And the more we tell them, the more powerful they become.'

'Trust me, I'd much rather believe that I'm the master of my own destiny — that I can overcome anything with the right mindset and a balanced diet — but that's just not my reality.'

'But what if it was? What if you told yourself a different story? Just this once. If the relationship is going to end regardless, what've you got to lose?'

'Everything. Don't you get it? If I allow myself to believe I won't lose her, even just for a second, it will crush me when I do.'

'But it's already crushing you, Theo. So why suffer twice?'

He had me there. Damn Hey-Jude and his pesky logic. I closed my eyes and took a deep breath before slowly exhaling in defeat.

'Fine. I'll pretend fairy tales are real and we'll live happily ever after.'

'That's the spirit!' Hey-Jude gave me an animated thumbs-up. 'But seriously, there's nothing wrong with pretending in the beginning. There's something to be said for faking it till you make it. Please promise me you'll try. If you give it your best shot, and the number still wins, I'll never suggest it again.'

'Okay, deal.'

We shook on it, and I swiftly changed the subject. 'Have the cops figured out who graffitied your car yet?'

'Surprisingly, yes. The perpetrator apologised and paid for the damage. So, you can retire, Sherlock. Case closed.'

'And that's it? Can't you press charges?'

'I'm not going to take a teenager to court over this.'

'Why not? Who is the jerk?'

'Just a cocky kid. He was bragging about it at school until someone reported him to the principal. Apparently, he even shared a picture of his masterpiece on social media. He's clearly not the sharpest tool in the shed.'

'Did he have any connection to Biddy?'

'Bridget Barker doesn't have a patent on discrimination,' Hey-Jude scoffed. 'But he goes to the same church, and when the cops asked him why he did it, he handed over one of Ms Barker's leaflets. So I guess she played her part.'

‘I knew it! Did they ban Biddy from spreading that homophobic trash around?’

‘They can’t. She’s within her rights, and a lot of people agree with her views on gay marriage and parenting, especially at our church.’

‘But it’s hate-mongering! How can you have faith in something that actively rejects you?’

‘God doesn’t reject me. God doesn’t reject anybody. That’s the whole point. Ms Barker has her interpretation and I have mine. But my family and I will no longer be attending a church that doesn’t embrace us.’

‘But your faith is important to you. You can’t let them chase you away.’

‘I’m not. It’s my choice. My family deserves better. From now on, we’ll be praying in a house of love. Because that’s what God is. Love. Community. Helping thy neighbour. We found a church that practises what it preaches. It welcomes everyone, regardless of their race or sexual orientation. It’s a longer drive. But it’s worth it.’

I felt positive leaving our session. If Hey-Jude could remain optimistic after all the shit he’s had to endure, the least I could do was try. I’m glad the bigots couldn’t extinguish Hey-Jude’s faith, though it pisses me off that he had to find another church. He’s been going to that church his whole life. Biddy should’ve been the one who had to change. But Hey-Jude seems satisfied. I guess that’s all that matters.

The positive vibes continued when I got home. Mom looked as though she'd been visited by the Fab Five in my absence. I'm talking full-on *Before and After* transformation. She was wearing a floral summer dress, and her hair was full and wavy. Makeup. Heels. The works.

'Mom?'

'Hi, honey. How'd things go with Dr Johnson?' She grabbed a glass of bubbly wine from the coffee table and took a sip.

'Um, fine . . . The cast of *Queer Eye* aren't in our kitchen, are they?'

'Don't be a smart-ass!'

I ignored her request. 'Because if they are, a heads-up would be nice. I can't meet Jonathan Van Ness with my hair looking like this.'

'Be serious. Is it too much?'

'I mean, it's a little fancy for day-drinking at home by yourself.'

'Very funny. I have a date, if you must know. He's picking me up any minute. I just needed a little liquid courage.'

This caught me off guard. I'd assumed she'd joined a new book club or something.

'In that case, you look beautiful.'

'Really, you don't think it's weird?'

'It's only weird that it's taken you this long. You

deserve to be happy. That's what Dad would want.'

I was gripped in a bear hug before I could say another word.

'Your dad would be so proud of the sweet, sensitive man you're becoming.'

I wriggled free. 'Who is this guy, anyway?'

'His name is Roy.' She blushed. 'We met at work. He's a regular. He's asked me out a few times but I was never ready. It wasn't until our talk the other day that I realised I needed to woman-up and take my own advice . . . Oh god! That'll be him!' She chugged her wine before scrambling for her purse and keys as the doorbell rang. 'Wish me luck!'

'You don't need it. You've got this. Just have fun.'

'Thanks, I've left pizza money on the counter. You should invite Lil over,' she said, shutting the door behind her.

I went to the window to get a look at this Roy fella. The only view I had was of his back when he opened the passenger door for Mom. Bonus points for chivalry.

'Please don't be a dick, Roy,' I thought aloud.

I TOOK MOM'S ADVICE and invited Lil over for pizza, even though I felt a bit nervous about it. We hadn't hung out in person since her last visit. And we know how that ended.

Hey 😊

I have a free house.

Fancy pizza and a movie?

Promise I won't throw a fit this time.

Twenty minutes went by. Nothing. Was our relationship really confined to the Realm again? I frantically checked my phone every 30 seconds as if I wouldn't hear it ping. I scrutinised every word of my text. I regretted mentioning the argument. Or that I had a free house. What if she thought I was implying something?

Luckily, my phone pinged before I puked.

Cool 😊

But I get 2 choose the movie.

U free in 30?

I replied quickly and ran upstairs to get changed, ransacking my wardrobe for a clean white tee to pair with black skinny jeans: my default setting. Casual but classic. I freshened up with mouthwash, sparingly applied some aftershave, attempted to style my hair but reconsidered. I shook my head, letting my hair fall back into its natural waves. The occasional washing and drying aside, my hair and I get on better the less I interfere.

By the time I'd given the living room a quick one-over and ordered the pizza, Lil was at the door. I was calm until I laid eyes on her, then my pulse skyrocketed. She was wearing a David Bowie tank top, ripped denim shorts and cherry Doc Martens. There was also something different about her. I'm a guy, so it took me a minute to figure it out. But it was her eyes. Her lashes were longer and darker, and framed with a smoky eyeshadow. I usually avoid people's eyes, for obvious reasons. But I've already seen her number — and besides, they are way too beautiful to be ignored.

I showed her through to the living room where I'd made some alterations to the furniture arrangement, pushing our leather two-seater closer to the TV and moving the coffee table into the middle for the pizza and snacks. I'd also dimmed the lights and closed the curtains to heighten the cinematic experience.

Lil took a seat while I grabbed a bottle of soda and some chips from the kitchen. I put everything on the coffee table, then sat down next to her. I could've sworn the couch had shrunk. Our legs brushed as I sat, and blood rushed to my cheeks. I prayed it stayed there. I placed a cushion on my lap in case it decided to head south.

'So, what movie do you wanna watch?'

She grinned and began humming a familiar theme tune as she reached for her bag. I knew the answer to my question before she pulled out the DVD.

'*Jurassic Park*. I should've guessed.'

'What else? It's only the greatest movie of all time.'

'Obviously,' I said. 'Just promise there will be no drooling over Jeff Goldblum.'

'I promise nothing of the sort. My salivary glands are slaves to his charm.'

'Okay, just keep it on your side of the couch, horndog.'

I put in the DVD and hit play.

Lil gave a chef's kiss as the opening music began. 'Best movie score ever!'

'Agreed.'

We watched the movie and passed the bag of chips back and forth until the pizza delivery guy arrived. Lil rubbed her hands in anticipation. 'What kind of pizza did you order?'

'Two Spicy Sweetcorn Supremes,' I answered.

'With extra jalapeños?'

'You know it!'

You'd swear I'd handed Lil a pot of gold when she opened the box. She inhaled deeply before sighing with pleasure.

'My favourite.'

'Oh, really?' I said nonchalantly. I already knew it was. She'd mentioned it once in the Realm. I'd tried it and became a convert.

'Do you have hot sauce?' she asked.

'Are you serious? It's pretty spicy.'

She smirked. 'Not to stereotype myself or anything, but I'm Mexican. And everyone knows the pizza joints in Fairview use white people chilies.'

I grabbed the spiciest sauce we had — which was probably mild by Lil's standards, though she didn't make a point about it. I added some to my pizza too so she wouldn't think I was a wimp. Combined with the jalapeños, it certainly packed a punch. But it was perfect. Gooey cheese, the girl of my dreams and dinosaurs. What more could a guy want?

Everything felt right. I didn't understand how watching a movie I'd already seen a hundred times could feel so epic. It was like I was seeing it for the first time. We laughed, jumped and marvelled at all the same parts. We were totally in sync — though she teared up during the scene where Sam Neill and Laura Dern see the Brachiosaurus for the first time. I've never wanted to hug anyone more.

When the movie was over, I poured us both a glass of wine. Mom had left almost a full bottle.

'Are you sure she won't mind?' Lil asked.

'I'm pretty sure she'd encourage it. She's always insisting I should be out partying at my age.'

'She seems cool. Is it weird that she's dating again?'

'No, it's actually kinda great. I want her to be happy, you know. The only weird part is the fact that my mom now has a more active dating life than me.'

Lil traced the rim of her glass with her finger. 'I'm sure that's not true. I bet you've broken plenty of hearts.'

My shoulders tensed up. If Lil knew I'd never been on a date, she'd think I was some kind of freak. I felt her eyes burning into me as she waited for my response.

Say something. Say anything. Lie, for Christ's sake. But nothing came out.

'Did you have a really bad break-up recently or something?' she prodded.

'Or something.' I gulped. My face was on fire. 'In order to have a break-up, I'd need to actually date someone first.'

'So, you've never had a serious relationship — big deal!'

'I've never even been on a date!'

I wanted to zip my lips together. Did Lil have the Lasso of Truth in her pocket?

'But you've been with a girl before, right?'

I sank back into the couch, wishing it would swallow me up.

'I had a crush on my friend Ally when I was 12. But she moved away.'

'And that's it?' She sounded genuinely surprised. 'You are too cute for that to be true.'

'And by cute you mean pathetic, right?'

She squinted at me like I was a puzzle she couldn't solve.

'No. I mean cute.'

Suddenly, everything slowed down. The space between us shrank until our faces were only millimetres apart. I wasn't sure which one of us was moving, but everything else blurred as her lips took focus. Before I knew it, we were kissing. She tasted like wine and chili. It was intoxicating. I'd only had a couple of sips of wine. But I felt drunk when she pulled away.

'Please tell me you weren't thinking about Jeff Goldblum,' I joked.

'Shut up!' She laughed before pulling me close again, gently biting my lip and kissing me more intensely than before.

Isn't life one effed-up Ferris wheel? A couple days ago I was crawling my way out of a hole. Now, I feel like I'm soaring sky high. I know what goes up must come down and maybe there'll be a reckoning. But right now I'm gonna enjoy the wind in my hair and admire the view.

CHAPTER FIFTEEN

LOVE IS A BATTLEFIELD — PAT BENATAR

I wasn't filled with my usual rage when I woke the next morning to the sound of crows squawking outside my window. It's no coincidence that the collective noun for a group of crows is a *murder*, because that's usually what I'd like to do to them. This morning, however, their incessant screeching sounded sweeter than Mozart's Serenade No. 13 in G Major. It's amazing how a little face smooshing can enhance your mood.

Believe it or not, red velvet curtains didn't descend from the heavens after Lil and I swapped saliva. Life isn't musical theatre, unfortunately. There was a little more to it than that.

Mom arrived home just as things were heating up. Lil and I shot to opposite ends of the couch the second the front door creaked, and we quickly composed ourselves while Mom and Roy giggled in the hallway.

'It's getting late. I should go,' Lil whispered.

'Do you have to?' I whispered back.

She kissed me one last time. 'See you tomorrow.'

I heard her say goodnight to Mom and Roy, but I stayed put, unsure whether I should go out and introduce myself to Roy or whether I could sneak up to my bedroom while he wasn't looking. This was uncharted territory. I didn't wanna scare the guy off, so decided the best course of action was to leave them be and flick through the channels. Eventually, I settled on *Game of Thrones*. But I wasn't paying attention. I was too busy thinking about Lil . . .

'*Game of Thrones*, sweet!'

I jumped at Roy's voice booming from behind me. He sounded like he was auditioning for Bill and Ted's next adventure.

'Theo?' Mom seemed less enthusiastic.

I looked up in horror as an explicit sex scene between Daenerys and Khal Drogo filled the screen.

'I wasn't watching that,' I blurted, fumbling for the remote.

'Why not? G-O-T rules, man!' Roy said, before taking a seat next to me and making himself at home.

'I'll get that coffee,' Mom said, disappearing to the kitchen.

I desperately wanted to follow her. But Roy was already high-fiving me. 'Sweet pad. Lynn is one seriously awesome chick.'

'Uh, thanks. I guess.'

Hearing this guy refer to my mom as a chick made me wanna barf.

'Lynnie tells me you're in college. Chicks dig a degree. Am I right?'

'You sure are,' I replied. *Right out of the dog pound.*

'You joined a fraternity house yet?'

'No, I've been busy fighting off all those bodacious college babes.'

'Right on,' Roy said, completely missing my sarcasm. 'In all seriousness, though, you need to join a frat. There's nothing more beautiful than a bunch of dudes becoming brothers. Frat bros are for life.'

Holy Keanu! Get this tool out of my house!

Roy, clearly oblivious to my irritation, proceeded to manspread. 'I still can't believe Lynnie has a kid. Must be gnarly having such a babe for a mom.'

He stretched his arms across the entire length of the sofa, and I suddenly felt like I was the guest in *his* home. What was Mom thinking? The guy reeked of cheap cologne and misogyny. Alarmed by the prospect of Roy asking me to call him Daddio one day,

I looked him dead in the eyes.

Hallelujah!

I've never been happier to see a pair of zeros in all my life.

But relief quickly turned to revulsion. Was this creep planning on ghosting my mom?

'I'm gonna see if *Lynnie* needs any help with the coffee,' I said, and rushed off to the kitchen to stage an intervention.

'Mom, I know I said I'm cool with you dating, but I'm really not comfortable with Roy spending the night,' I hissed.

'*What*?' Mom erupted, before dialing it back to a whisper. 'Roy is *not* spending the night!'

I let out a mammoth sigh. 'Oh, thank Keanu!'

'I've been trying to ditch him all night. But he insisted on coming back for coffee.'

I felt bad for having questioned Mom's intelligence. Of course she was trying to ditch this asshole. And of course he refused to take the hint. Roy was obviously that special brand of creep that thinks the word *no* is a suggestion. Luckily, I had a plan.

'Nuff said,' I told her, and confidently marched back to the living room.

'Is it true? Is it really true?' I shouted, galloping towards Roy like an excited puppy.

'Is what true, kid?'

'Mom said you're my new Daddy!'

'Huh?'

The look of horror on his face was priceless. I wish I'd taken a photo.

'You wanna see the taxidermy room?' I asked, grabbing his hand.

Roy squirmed his way to freedom and was already halfway out the door when Mom returned with the coffee.

'On second thoughts, I'll skip the coffee, babe. Gives me the runs.'

'Charming,' Mom said.

He was gone before she could ask what was going on.

'Do I even want to know?' she said, then erupted with laughter when I told her what I'd done. 'Theodore Brown, you are evil! What on earth am I going say the next time I see him?'

'I have a feeling you won't be seeing old Roy anytime soon,' I replied smugly.

Mom handed me a cup of coffee, and we dissolved into another fit of laughter.

'I'm sorry your date was a bust,' I said when I'd finally caught my breath.

'Don't be. I haven't laughed this hard in a long time.'

'You're not disappointed?'

She took a sip of coffee while she pondered this.

'Honestly, no. For the longest time I couldn't even

begin to imagine dating again. I still have no clue what I'm looking for in a guy. But it ain't Roy. I know that much. So, I guess I'm closer to figuring out what I do want.'

I smiled. 'I guess we're both making progress then.'

We clinked our coffee mugs together in solidarity.

'To progress,' Mom said. 'I take it things went better with Lil this time?'

'Yeah. It was kinda perfect actually.'

'That's wonderful, honey. She seems lovely.'

'She's the best,' I agreed. And that was as much as I wanted to divulge for now.

But I couldn't stop thinking about our kiss and what it potentially meant.

It certainly didn't feel like a pity-kiss. It seemed like she was into it. Like she was into me. But I couldn't be sure, given my lack of experience in the matter. Still, I knew it was too soon to throw a parade. That would have to wait till I'd confirmed it wasn't a fluke. Then, we could break out the marching band. Drums, tubas, trumpets, the works! An entire 100-piece orchestra to explode into 'Call Me Maybe' by Carly Rae Jepsen.

For now, I've reverted to my default setting: over-thinking. I desperately want to text Lil, but don't want to seem clingy. On the other hand, if I leave it too long, she might think I'm not interested anymore. There's a fine line between playing it cool and being a jerk. I'm just not exactly sure *where* that line is.

CHAPTER SIXTEEN

BOYFRIEND — TEGAN AND SARA

This just in: tamales are the bomb! In other, perhaps more pressing news, Lil and I are dating! Officially. IRL. This isn't a drill. And it's not April first.

That's right, Theodore Brown, former wallflower and self-proclaimed social pariah, might be on his way to being Lil's boyfriend. I didn't need to worry about playing it cool after all. I got a text from Lil around lunchtime yesterday.

How was breakfast with Roy? Lol 😆

Lil couldn't have spent more than 60 seconds with the guy. But he still managed to make a lasting impression. Apparently, Roy also struggles with eye contact. Lil said she needed to take a shower after he thoroughly ogled her in the hallway. You gotta give the guy props: he could teach a class on how to repel a woman in under a minute.

Awesome, he's teaching me how to play baseball today.

Seriously???

Hell no! He bolted shortly after you. I'm pretty sure I scarred him for life.

What???

Long story. Fill you in later.
What u up to?

Making tamales.

It pains me to admit that I had to ask what a tamale is. Turns out it's a traditional Mesoamerican dish containing seasoned meat (or veggies in Lil's case) wrapped in cornmeal dough and steamed in a corn husk. They're also the most delicious thing I've ever put in my mouth. Lil wasn't having it when I told her I'd never tried one.

Are you serious? Get
over here ASAP! I'm
poppin ur tamale cherry!

I'm so down 4 that. Ur
parents cool with me
coming over?

They r @ work.

Now get ur butt over here, philistine.

Ur about to have ur tastebuds blown.

Had I hit the jackpot or what? Lil plus food minus parental supervision equalled the Holy Grail in my book.

THE MOMENT I ARRIVED at Lil's house, it felt completely different from how it was the first time. It was like any walls we'd built between us had been demolished. A lifetime of disappointments and their accompanying defence mechanisms had been dismantled with a kiss. Now that the sexual tension had been addressed, we were free to be ourselves. We'd shed our flaky old skins and become something new. Something smooth and poised. Talking, touching, kissing — they all felt as natural as breathing. Like this was how we were supposed to be all along.

Lil took me by the hand as soon as she opened the door. She marched me straight to the kitchen, which looked like one of those swanky TV sets you see on the Food Network — all marble surfaces, fancy flower arrangements and shiny new appliances. I couldn't have told you what half of them were even for. But they made our kitchen at home look like something from *The Flintstones*.

On one of the gleaming benches Lil had laid out all the ingredients needed for my cherry popping. The recipe had been in her family for generations, she told me, but she'd modified it to suit her vegetarian diet. Otherwise the recipe was older than dirt. Sharing it with me felt oddly intimate.

After a very quick cooking tutorial, Lil put me to work. She runs a tight kitchen. I'm not gonna lie, it was kinda hot.

'Easy there, tiger! Not so heavy with the masa dough,' she commanded, smacking my hand with a wooden spoon. 'Remember your training, rookie. Just three table-spoons per corn husk.'

'Yes, Chef!'

Once we'd finished spreading the husks with masa dough, it was time to add the filling. I could've quite happily eaten an entire bowl of that by itself.

'You're gonna lose that finger if you're not careful,' Lil teased when she caught me finger-dipping.

'What's in this again?' I asked, paying more attention now that I'd tasted literal perfection.

Lil listed each of the ingredients on her fingers. 'Corn, tomatoes, jalapeños, cilantro, queso fresco, pinto beans and a generous pinch of my abuela's secret spice blend.'

I was drooling. 'Why does it smell so good?'

'That'll be the secret spice blend.'

'What's in it?'

'You've already seen too much. If I told you that I'd have to kill you. And that'd be a waste. You're way too good at kissing.'

I could feel myself blushing to the roots of my hair. I haven't been told I'm good at anything besides writing. I never imagined I'd add kissing to the list.

'Can I have one more spoonful?' I pleaded.

She dipped her finger into the bowl and held a dollop of filling up to my mouth. 'This is all you're getting. You'll spoil your appetite, man-child.'

I licked the filling off Lil's finger. Suddenly, food was the last thing on my mind. But Lil was all business. Once we finished adding the filling to the remaining corn husks, she showed me how to fold and tie them. She leaned over me and gently guided my hands. The smell of her perfume turned my legs to silly string.

'Now we've just gotta steam them for an hour.'

'An hour!' I groaned.

She pulled me close, gently biting my lip. 'I'm sure we can find a way to pass the time.'

She grabbed my hand again and dragged me to the lounge. Flustered as I was by her touch, I couldn't help but be dazzled by the sheer size of the place. This room was bigger than the entire ground floor of my house. An ornate crystal chandelier dangled from a ridiculously high ceiling. Towering white bookcases and framed family portraits lined the walls. Everything was pristine. But it was kind of cold, too. I couldn't see Lil in any of the portraits. She was in every one of them, of course; I just didn't recognise her. Her hair was too neat, and she looked stiff and robotic. Who was this prim and proper princess modelling a line of demure dresses with matching cardigans in inoffensive pastels? I'd never met this version of Lil. I could see the discomfort beneath each forced smile. She was giving off Stepford Wife on the verge of malfunctioning.

'Please ignore those,' Lil said, following my gaze.

'How did your parents bribe you into posing for these?'

'Let's just say art supplies aren't cheap.'

She clearly didn't want to say more, because she pushed me onto a stiff velvet couch and kissed me hungrily.

A regular guy could've happily spent the entire hour making out. But something was gnawing at me and it wasn't long before Lil sensed something was off.

'What's up? Are you bored of me already?'

'No! Absolutely, positively not. I could do this forever . . . I was just wondering . . . what this means . . . to you.'

She sat up straight, brushing her hair from her face.

'What do you want it to mean?'

'I dunno. Something, I guess,' I said, suddenly unsure of myself.

'Well, it definitely means something,' she declared, before diving back in for round two.

'So are we dating?' I blurted.

Lil hesitated, and I wanted to shrink until I entered the quantum realm.

'No,' she said after careful consideration. 'Right now, we're making out. For us to be dating, we'd need to go on an actual date first.'

I'm such an idiot!

'Right, of course . . . but I mean . . . is that . . . something you'd . . . maybe . . . wanna—'

Thankfully, she responded before I mumbled my way into oblivion. 'Holy cow, yes! I'll go on a date with you. Just don't short-circuit on me.'

'Cool.' I grinned goofily like she'd just injected me with morphine.

'You're such a nerd,' she teased, before pinning me down again.

Now that she'd put my mind at ease, I relaxed and enjoyed her soft lips pressing against mine. I felt like the luckiest nerd alive.

Until her parents arrived home.

Lil shot up at the sound of their car pulling up in the driveway. 'Shit! They're home early.'

She leapt off the couch and frantically straightened her hair and clothes.

'Something smells good!' came a deep male voice from the hallway.

I'd assumed it was merely a coincidence that I hadn't met her parents. But Lil was visibly uncomfortable as their footsteps drew nearer.

'Lily, there you are,' Mrs Sanchez said as she swept into the room. 'You didn't tell us you were having a *friend* over.'

She and her husband looked just like their portraits. Regal and sharply dressed, like they'd just returned from the theatre or some fancy country club. But they could've been grocery shopping for all I knew. They seemed like the kind of people who are always photo ready.

'It was a last-minute thing,' Lil replied unconvincingly. 'This is Theo, the friend I was telling you about.'

Mr Sanchez looked me up and down suspiciously like I might be concealing a weapon in my pocket. To him, I guess I was. 'The boy from the video game?'

'Yes, Papá. But he doesn't actually live inside the video game,' Lil replied dryly. 'He lives down the street.'

'Then why are we only meeting him now?' Mr Sanchez asked.

'We've only just met outside the Realm recently, sir,' I said. 'It's nice to meet you. You have a beautiful home.'

'Gracias, that's very sweet,' Mrs Sanchez replied.

'I hope that means you'll both be spending less time glued to your computer screens,' Mr Sanchez added. 'It's becoming a real mission to coax Lil out of her dungeon.'

'The basement isn't a dungeon, Papá. It's my only creative space in this entire house. Besides, at least you know where I am. I could be out partying or doing drugs! You should be happy that I'm playing video games and painting.'

'Will you be staying for lunch, Theo?' Mrs Sanchez interrupted. I got the impression she was used to playing referee. 'Smells like Lil's been cooking tamales.'

'That's why he's here,' Lil said. 'Theo has *never* had tamales! Isn't that the saddest thing you've ever heard?'

'A real tragedy indeed,' Mr Sanchez nodded.

'I'm afraid I've had a somewhat sheltered diet,' I said.

'It's not your fault,' Lil said. 'The closest thing Fairview has to Mexican food is Taco Bell, or as Papá likes to call it Taco Hell!'

Mr Sanchez smiled. 'Please, that soulless franchise is about as Mexican as McDonalds.'

Mrs Sanchez rolled her eyes as if she'd heard this a million times. 'Come on, mi vida,' she said, dragging Mr Sanchez away. 'Let's leave the kids in peace.'

'That's okay,' Lil said. 'We were about to head to my *dungeon* anyways. We'll be back up when the tamales are ready.' And with that she grabbed me by my shirt and led me to the basement.

'Don't forget to leave the door open down there, Lily!' Mr Sanchez bellowed after us.

'Seriously!' Lil yelled back. 'Papá, we're just friends!'

'Then you won't mind leaving the door open,' he replied.

Touché, Mr Sanchez.

But Lil wasn't done. 'That's not the point! I'm 18 — I'm entitled to a little privacy.'

'You can have all the privacy you want when you move out. Until then, my roof, my rules.'

'Ugh! Anything else I can do for you, King Tritan?'

'Love you,' Mr Sanchez said.

'Tolerate you,' Lil replied.

I figured this was a frequent exchange between the two.

'Just friends, huh?' I teased. 'Burn!'

'Would you rather I told my intensely overprotective father that you're *Frenching* his only daughter?'

I took a second to consider this. 'I'm good.'

Back in the basement, Lil showed me her latest sketches. Drawing is like a supernatural power if you ask me. How Lil was able to create a dystopian world in her mind and then project it onto paper in photo-realistic detail was a complete mystery. I was in total awe.

'They're just rough designs I've been toying with for a video game concept,' she said nonchalantly. 'They're not finished yet.'

I couldn't see how she could possibly improve them. There was so much beauty and pathos in the ravaged landscapes she'd created.

'Are you kidding? They're perfect.'

Lil gnawed at her index fingernail. 'Not yet, but they will be after a bit of fine-tuning.'

'Has your dad seen these?'

'Look around,' Lil said, gesturing to the walls. Every inch was plastered with her artwork. 'I'm not exactly discreet about where my passion lies.'

'Then how can he believe you belong in business school?'

'He just wants me to succeed. My father grew up dirt poor. He worked his ass off for everything we have. He reminds me daily of how privileged I am. And he's not wrong. I admire the hell out of him. But our ideas of success are different, and sometimes that drives me crazy.'

'Your art could make you the biggest thing to come out of Fairview. There's more than one path to success.'

'Not according to Papá. In his eyes, knowledge is power, time is money and drawing is a hobby.'

'No offence, but he's wrong. This is what you were born to do.'

'Thanks. I'll be sure to pass that along to him.'

'Please don't. Your dad is scary, and I really want him to like me.'

Lil smiled. 'I see, and why might that be?'

'Because I really like you.'

'And I really like you too. Which means my father will inevitably disapprove.' She shrugged. 'But hey, that's par for the course.'

We gamed until the tamales were ready, but it was a struggle to keep my eyes on the screen. I was wonderstruck by Lil's artwork. It would be a crime against humanity if her talent went to waste — although something told me she had too much fire to let that happen.

The tamales were undoubtedly the best thing I've ever eaten. All in all, it was a damn near perfect day. There was just one little thing that bothered me. After we'd eaten, I asked Lil if she'd started reading *Timothy's Terrible Time Machine*. She said she'd been too busy with her art, which was fair. But that book means a lot to me. Giving it to her was like sharing a part of my soul. I'd made an effort with her stuff. I'd listened to all her favourite artists and legitimately become a fan. I was hurt she hadn't made the effort to reciprocate.

I'm probably overthinking it. She'll get around to it soon, I'm sure. Besides, I've got bigger fish to fry. I need to ask Lil out on a real date to make this official. Trouble is, I've gotta figure out what people do on dates. I don't want to be boring and predictable, and you only get one shot at a first date. I want all our firsts to be epic.

CHAPTER SEVENTEEN

ONLY YOU — THE FLYING PICKETS

You know that scene from *Bambi* — the one where he tries to walk across the frozen pond? For anyone who hasn't seen it, picture a gangly little fawn learning to walk for the first time — but on ice! That pretty much sums up my first date with Lil. I'm Bambi, the pond is our first date and Lil is Thumper, the poor rabbit tasked with keeping Bambi on his feet.

Mom said I simply had to be myself and Lil would fall head over heels. Yeah, right. No one is as special or charming as their mother perceives them to be. She also suggested opening doors and paying for dinner, but I worried that might be construed as sexist in the modern dating world. I mean, Lil is more than capable of opening doors and paying for her own dinner. She's much smarter and richer than I am. But would I look like a scrub if I didn't? I hate catch-22s.

The internet wasn't much help either. Don't get me wrong, I love a good googling as much as the next guy. But I've learned two things: the internet should never be used for dating or medical advice. Like, do people really go skydiving on a first date? And what's with manscaping? Do we collectively hate pubic hair now? And don't get me started on the comment sections . . . it's a scary world we live in. I was starting to think it might be safer to die alone.

Thankfully, I can always count on Hey-Jude. His advice was foolproof. It's just a shame that on this occasion I wasn't smart enough to take it. He suggested I choose an activity that incorporated both of our interests. Something to do with old movies, art or video games. Logical. Simple. Thoughtful. Naturally, I ignored this and did the complete opposite.

What can I say? I crumble under pressure. I became so consumed with trying to figure out what girls like, I totally forgot what Lil likes. That's the most frustrating part. Because if I'd only focused on that, I would've knocked our first date out of the park.

I didn't screw up the entire evening. I managed to pick her up without a single hitch. Mom even let me borrow the car. And Lil looked amazing as always. She wore a black denim pinafore dress with a striped turtleneck underneath and her trademark cherry Doc Martens. I didn't scrub up so bad myself. I rocked my dad's vintage leather jacket with a white button-down shirt and blue jeans. Lil said I looked like an old Hollywood star. I must've been channeling my inner James Dean.

Lil's parents said we looked awfully fancy for two friends *hanging out*. I'm almost certain they knew it was a date. After a few awkward pleasantries on their porch, Lil and I made a speedy exit before they could grill us further.

'What's with all the mystery, Agatha Christie?' Lil asked as she got into the car.

I'd decided it would be more romantic if the date was a surprise.

'All will be revealed in due course, Nancy Drew,' I quipped.

She grumbled before turning on the radio. 'Only You' by The Flying Pickets was playing. It was the perfect song for a first date. She put her hand on my thigh and sang along. I instantly regretted wearing skinny jeans. They are not designed to hide erections. Luckily, Lil seemed too busy vibing with the music to notice. She has the cutest singing voice. She's not gonna win any contests, that's for sure, but I love that she sings at the top of her lungs anyway. Her pitchy vocals and zero fucks attitude are enough to make anyone smile.

I knew Lil was disappointed when we reached our destination: the Fairview Botanical Gardens. You'd swear by the look on her face we'd pulled into the city dump. But I was hopeful she'd come around when she saw the epic picnic basket I'd prepared, no expense spared. It had fancy cheese and crackers, breadsticks, hummus, strawberries, sparkling wine and that posh tapenade stuff she likes. I'd even scoped out the gardens to find the perfect picnic spot under a magnificent old red maple right by a pond dotted with water lilies. I was sure I'd aced it. But as I laid the picnic blanket down and set everything up, it dawned on me that Lil hadn't said a word since we left the car.

'Is everything all right?' I asked. 'Did I get the wrong tapenade?'

'No, it's great. Thank you.'

I wasn't convinced. She avoided eye contact when she spoke. And it's a bad sign when I notice lack of eye contact.

'It's a nice spot, right?' I said, gazing out at the pond.

She nodded. 'It's pretty.'

But I sensed apathy rather than agreement.

'You're still the prettiest Lily here though.'

Lil winced.

'Did I do something wrong?' I asked.

'What is all this? You know I don't like when people call me Lily!'

'I was trying to be romantic. Besides, it's your name, isn't it? Why do you hate it so much?'

I genuinely wanted to know. I'd never seen someone look disgusted by the sound of their own name.

'Because that's what my parents want me to be — their perfect little flower. But that's not me. And it never will be! So, if that's what you want too, this isn't gonna work!'

Her words came out in short sharp bursts. I wanted to hug her. But I knew that wasn't what she needed right now. She wanted me to see her. The real her.

'I promise that's not what I want. I don't see you as a flower, Lil. You're the whole damn garden. Thorns and all. You're stubborn, and bossy, and passionate, and creative, and smart, and funny . . . and you're the best at video games — like, you're literally undefeatable. It's scary. You're also the most talented artist I know, and I don't want you to be anything less. I'm crazy about you.'

Her eyes glistened. I was worried she might cry. But she was smiling.

'This just doesn't feel like us.'

'You're right,' I agreed. 'I screwed up.'

'No, you're sweet. It's my fault. I've never been good at *sweet*.'

'And you don't have to be. You're good at a million other things. You don't have to be anything other than yourself with me.'

She wrapped her arms around me, and I finally felt like I'd done something right.

'I think I might be crazy about you too, Theodore Brown.'

Then she kissed me, or maybe I kissed her. It was one of those all-consuming instances where the universe seems to take the wheel.

'Can we have a do-over?' I asked, panting as I came up for air. 'I don't want this to be our first date.'

'Absolutely not! This is perfect.'

'But I thought you said—'

'Ignore me, I'll never forget this . . . But we could always extend the date.'

'What did you have in mind?'

'They're playing a *Dracula* double feature at FairFlix.'

Damn it, Janet! Why didn't I think of that?

'With Bela Lugosi?'

'Obviously,' Lil smiled.

The rest of the evening was perfect. We felt more at home in a darkened theatre than in the botanical gardens. There's something magical about the combination of red velvet chairs, the smell of fresh popcorn and a black-and-white movie. We held hands and watched in wonder as Bela Lugosi took us under his thrall.

This was *us*. Two dorks fangirling in the dark.

It was late when we left the theatre. The air was crisp, and every star in the galaxy was visible in the sky. The existence of vampires seemed almost plausible under the glorious full moon. We were too buzzed to go home. So, we drove around aimlessly, discussing our favourite monster movies and why black-and-white cinema needs to make a comeback. When I parked outside Lil's house, the conversation became more intimate.

'So, now that we've got our awkward first date out of the way, does this mean we're officially dating?' I asked.

Lil grinned. 'Technically, it was two dates. So, I'd say we're dating aficionados at this point.'

'The latter half was infinitely more fun. I'm sorry about earlier.'

'Don't you dare apologise. The botanical gardens were the best part.'

'You're kidding?'

'No. What you said — that was the sweetest thing anyone's ever said to me.'

So, I didn't mess up so badly after all. I somehow managed to get it right by getting it totally wrong. Or maybe I'm just getting really good at digging myself out of holes. Either way, I'm dating the coolest person in the world. How did that happen?

CHAPTER EIGHTEEN

HOT TO GO! — CHAPPELL ROAN

It's been over a month since my first date with Lil. We've been pretty much inseparable ever since, and I've been savouring every second of our blissful honeymoon period while it lasts. I still can't believe it, but . . . she's my girlfriend now! I feel like I've won the life lottery.

And that's not the only news. Something pretty big happened. Monumental, one might say. I lost my virginity!

It all started with a trip to the Bahamas — for Lil's parents, that is. They decided to celebrate their twentieth wedding anniversary with a romantic Caribbean getaway. Meaning Lil had a free house for the entire week. My phone buzzed as soon as she got the news.

Yo Goober, guess what?

You've finally found a cuter pet name for me?

No ur still a Goober. But I hav a free house this week!!!

Cool. U planning a wild party or something?

Eww! Gross. Do u even know me?

Then wats with the triple-exclamation-level excitement?

Hmmm . . . Why wud a teenage girl b excited about having a free house with her hot new boyfrend? I wonder . . . 😉

I gulped. How was I supposed to respond to that? Was she insinuating what I thought? I had to be getting ahead of myself. Surely. But there was a winky face! What did that mean? Then my phone buzzed again.

U could spend the night. The week even. I'm sure we can find something better to do than some cliché teen party. 😉😉

Double winky face! She meant business.

I'm sure we can. Sounds hot!

Sounds hot? Seriously! What am I, Paris Hilton? Thankfully, I had enough sense to delete the fire emoji before I hit send. But I was still flooded with regret. I was aiming for cool and nonchalant. Fail! I dived headfirst into a full panic spiral. Was it presumptuous to think Lil was suggesting we have sex? We were still on first base. Spending the night could mean a multitude of things. This didn't mean she wanted to go all the way. But what if she did?

I wasn't sure if I was ready. Heck, I wasn't even sure I knew how. Okay, I'm not an idiot. I knew *how*. But that doesn't mean I knew how to be good at it. I knew she was more experienced than me — let's face it, who wasn't? Oddly, there was some relief in this. At least one of us would have a clue what we were doing. I wasn't going to torture myself by conjuring images of her potential ex-lovers to compare myself to. No one wants to be that guy. I knew that much. I just didn't want to disappoint her.

Yet again, I found myself in need of advice. I was too embarrassed to talk to Hey-Jude about sex, and I sure as hell wasn't gonna ask Mom. She'd given me the obligatory *birds and bees* spiel and we'd been taught basic sex ed in school. But I didn't need help with the logistics. Why doesn't anyone tell you about technique, or what feels good, or how to last longer than a minute? Were we supposed to just know this stuff? Because I knew squat. I knew I had to wear a condom and which orifice to put it in. But that was the extent of my knowledge. And I knew the internet was unlikely to be of any help. I'd learned that the hard way after my first-date faux pas, and I'm smart enough to realise that porn is not real life. Women rarely look like they're having a good time in those videos. Granted, I'm basing this on my very limited exposure to porn, but I'd seen enough to know I wasn't going to find any answers there. I wanted sex to mean something. Especially my first time. I wanted Lil to enjoy it as much as I did.

So, I decided I wasn't gonna make the same mistake twice. If I needed to know what Lil liked, I'd simply ask her when the time came.

WHEN I TOLD MOM I was spending the week at Lil's, I braced myself for the third degree. But she was surprisingly chill, aside from asking me if we were being *careful.* I shrugged her off and told her she had nothing to worry about. Miraculously, this was all the reassurance she needed.

Meanwhile, I'd got so hung up with performance anxiety, I forgot to buy condoms. I still didn't know if we'd actually need them — but it was better to be prepared. I figured I'd need them *some day* in the future. Unfortunately, this epiphany didn't hit me until about 10 minutes before I was due to meet Lil. Still, I managed to keep my cool: I could pick some up at FairPrice while Lil was at the liquor store across the street. She wanted to grab some supplies before heading back to her place. Her parents were trusting but they still locked the liquor cabinet.

I was a bundle of nerves by the time we met. But Lil planted a glossy, peach-flavoured kiss on my cheek as she hopped into the passenger seat, and I quickly settled.

'Are you ready for a weekend of unsupervised, uninterrupted, uncensored bliss?' she howled.

I raised my eyebrows. Who was this girl and what had she done with Lil?

'You sound like the beginning of a bad spring break movie,' I said.

'Whatever,' she scoffed. 'You're not gonna kill my buzz. I love my parents. But I'll love them even more from afar. Now take me to the booze.'

She had a fake ID like any self-respecting under-age drinker. I didn't, so that provided the perfect excuse for me to run across the road and grab the snacks while she hit the liquor store.

No biggie, I told myself upon entering FairPrice. People buy condoms all the time. The way guys talked at college, I felt like the only one who wasn't ploughing through a box a week. But the supermarket seemed brighter and busier than usual. I grabbed a basket and filled it with a random assortment of chips, soda and candy in a desperate attempt to conceal my real objective. When I reached the aisle where the contraceptives were shelved, I was startled by the variety. I panic-grabbed the most discreet-looking pack and buried it among my other hasty purchases. I had no idea if I'd even got the right size.

At the checkout, I casually placed my basket on the conveyor belt and pulled out my phone as if replying to a text. The cashier looked a couple of years younger than me. I could feel my cheeks start to burn as he quickly scanned and bagged the contents of my basket.

'That'll be 29 dollars,' he said in a monotone.

That wasn't so bad, I thought as I handed over the cash. 'Thanks, have a great weekend.'

The guy flashed his shiny braces at me with a knowing smirk. 'Likewise. Have fun, dude.'

I felt icky. I grabbed the grocery bag and hurried back to the car, quickly removing the condoms en route. I put one in my wallet and pushed the box to the bottom of the bag. I'd stash them in my rucksack when I got to Lil's.

Lil was casually leaning on the back of the car. She laughed when she spotted the bag bursting with sugar and MSG.

'Dude, do you have the munchies? You know we've got food at my place, right?'

'I like to be prepared,' I said, no pun intended. 'Did your ID pass the test?'

'Always. I got red *and* white, since I don't know which you prefer.'

Honestly, I prefer beer but knew I'd be thankful for the extra-strength Dutch courage later.

Lil seemed chill but I almost blew the whole thing with my not-so-subtle attempt at reconnaissance on the drive back to her house.

'So, you ever had a guy spend the night before?' I blurted.

She glared at me. 'If you're asking whether I've had sex with a guy, the answer is no.'

'Really?'

'Is that a huge shock to you or something?'

'No, I didn't mean it like that. I guess I just assumed I was the only virgin left in Fairview.'

She paused. 'I never said I was a virgin,' she said.

I was momentarily flummoxed — until I had one of those *Aha!* moments Oprah is always yapping about.

'Ohhh! Sorry, I just assumed . . . Have you always known you were bi?'

'Not exactly, but I've never identified as straight. I'm a little weird about labels, to be honest. I think sexuality can evolve and change over time, and how I identify today might not necessarily fit who I am tomorrow, ya know?'

Surprisingly I did know. Deep down, I think I've always felt a similar way. I just needed to hear someone articulate it.

'Yeah, I'm not sure anyone's 100 percent gay or straight,' I said. 'I think everyone must experiment or fantasise about it at some point in their lives.'

It's almost like I was waiting for permission to say it aloud, and with Lil I felt like I could say anything.

Lil's eyes doubled in size. 'I'm sensing a story. Spill the tea, Brown.'

'There's no tea. You're literally the first person I've ever dated.'

She clearly wasn't satisfied with my answer. 'Okay, but something must've sparked this enlightened view.'

I shrugged. 'I figure it's only natural. People are curious by nature. We're just conditioned to suppress same-sex attractions.'

'And who ignited your curiosity?'

'No one. Like I said, it's not like I have a ton of experience.'

'But you have eyes. You have fantasies, don't you?'

I'd backed myself into a corner, and there was no way she was gonna let this bone go.

'Okay, fine,' I said. 'But if I tell you something, you have to promise not to make fun of me.'

She perked up like an inquisitive meerkat. 'Cross my heart.'

'Don't get too excited. It's more embarrassing than interesting.'

'This is a safe space. There's no judgement here. Now, spill it, Brown!'

'Well, when I first started, you know . . .'

'Figure skating?' she quipped.

'You promised you wouldn't make fun!'

She threw her hands in the air. 'Sorry. Continue, I'll be good.'

'When I first started . . . masturbating, I got off to some pretty eclectic material.'

'Such as?'

'Promise you won't laugh?'

She zipped her lips and held out her pinky. I wrapped my pinky around hers, and we formed a binding contract of secrecy.

'Sometimes, not always, but occasionally . . . my eyes would wander to my James Dean poster as I . . . climaxed.'

She struggled not to giggle. I could tell. She bit her lower lip to hold her mouth closed. But she was true to her word. She didn't laugh or judge.

'Do you still want me to stay over?' I asked.

'No, Theo. I'm a homophobic bisexual. Pull over, I'm gonna vomit!'

'Asshole!'

'Cutey,' she replied with a kiss.

Her laidback response was exactly what I needed. It hadn't been the conversation I'd anticipated, but having her acknowledge that my attraction to guys was normal felt amazing. I'd never spoken about anything like this before, not even in therapy. I'd done a pretty good job at concealing it from myself, to be honest. But the more I got to know Lil, the more I knew myself. She never pretended to be anyone other than herself, and I didn't want to pretend anymore either. I wanted her to know me. All of me.

When we reached her house, she bounced out of the car and up the driveway as if nothing had changed. This was comforting but also a bit jarring. A lot had changed for me already. But I trailed after her with my bags and decided to go with the flow. I knew I'd be on cloud nine no matter what she had planned for the rest of the day.

First thing on the agenda: gaming — our safe place.

We played for a few hours before Lil announced that it was my turn to cook. I hadn't been prepared for that and didn't have a bunch of vegetarian recipes in my arsenal, but I was pretty sure I could pull off a quick version of Mom's famous veggie lasagna — I'd watched her make it often enough and had the assistance of Casa del Sanchez's well-stocked pantry. It didn't turn out quite as good as Mom's, but Lil was impressed.

IT WASN'T TILL AFTER dinner and several glasses of wine that I mustered up the courage to follow up on the conversation we'd had in the car.

‘So, tell me more about this mystery girl,’ I asked. ‘Was she someone special?’

Lil side-eyed me like I’d just farted at the dinner table. ‘Have you been ruminating over that all day, perv?’

‘No! Okay, maybe a little. But not in a creepy way. I just wondered if it was serious?’

Lil paused to measure my sincerity. ‘It was to me,’ she said softly. There was a despondency in her voice that I’d never heard before.

‘I’m sorry,’ I said, suddenly feeling like an insensitive jerk.

‘It’s not your fault. I guess it’s natural you’d be curious. I did sorta spring it on you.’

‘I’m glad you did,’ I said, wanting to reassure her. ‘The more I know, the more I like you.’

She smiled and looked away, tracing the rim of her wine glass with her index finger. ‘There’s not much to tell really. We met in senior year. She’d just moved here from California. Everyone loved her immediately. She was pretty and popular — all the usual cliché high school bullshit. Every guy in school bent over backwards to be near her. But while the boys ogled her, she was busy checking me out. At first, I thought it was in my head. I couldn’t understand why she’d be interested in me. Hell, I never thought I’d be interested in someone like her. She looked like a living Barbie.

But she was sweet and smart, and we quickly became besties. It was weird. But she made me feel like I could do anything, you know?'

'Yeah, I think I do,' I said.

'Anyway, one day she asked if I wanted to have a sleepover at her place. Just me and her. Obviously, I jumped at the chance. I'd been fantasising about it for months. I still didn't know if she liked me back — but the sleepover cleared that up. Let's just say she wasn't interested in talking about boys or braiding each other's hair. Pretty soon, these sleepovers became a regular thing. I fell hard. And I thought she felt the same. Turns out we were on two very different pages of two very different books. I thought we were dating. But for her we were just *messing around*.'

'Ouch!'

'She made this crystal clear when she started dating Grant Baldwin, resident quarterback and total meathead. I felt like I was in a bad teen drama. She begged me not to tell anyone about us. She said she'd deny it if I did and that nobody would believe me anyway. Obviously, I told her to go screw herself, and we never spoke again. Sometimes, I honestly think I dreamed the whole thing up.'

'Wow! That's rough.'

My words felt inadequate. But I didn't know what else to say.

'That's life,' Lil said, sounding blasé.

But I could tell it still stung a little.

'Do you ever regret sleeping with her?'

She looked surprised. 'Never. Why?'

'Doesn't it suck? Getting close to someone. Sharing the most intimate parts of yourself, only to lose them completely. How do you move on from that?'

Lil shrugged. 'You just do. As sucky as it was losing her, we weren't right for each other. Not in the long run. But that doesn't mean what we had wasn't meaningful. I learned a ton about myself, sexually and emotionally. I wouldn't be this version of me if I hadn't met her.'

As her words sank in, something inside of me began to shift. The world was much less scary through Lil's eyes.

'Are you okay?' she asked.

I wanted to tell her I was more than okay. But instead I asked if I could kiss her.

'Yeah, but not here. Let's go upstairs.'

BEING A GUY IS hard sometimes. Pun intended. I had a boner before we reached Lil's bedroom. I knew enough to know that speed was not going to be an asset in this scenario. I needed to be the tortoise, not the hare. Unfortunately, my penis had no appreciation for the wisdom of Aesop's Fables.

Lil's bedroom was a cross between the creative chaos of the basement and the carefully curated aesthetic of the rest of the house. It wasn't devoid of personality. Her artistic energy was sprinkled throughout. Sketch pads and art books were stacked neatly on her desk. A couple of her paintings in white wooden frames dressed the walls, and there was a large watercolour of Dolly Parton hanging above her bed.

'That's amazing,' I said.

'Dolly is about the only thing my parents and I agree on.'

'You can always count on Dolly to bring people together. I swear, that woman is magic.'

'Oh, she's a witch, for sure!'

Lil's bed looked pristine, like it had never been ruffled, let alone slept in. It had more cushions than my entire house, all perfectly arranged by size. I was afraid to sit down. Suddenly, Lil pushed the cushions onto the floor, pinned me down and was kissing me madly. I was totally enveloped in her. Her scent was everywhere. All I could do was surrender to the moment. Completely. It was ecstasy.

She tore my clothes off like they were nothing but a silly costume. Strangely, I didn't feel insecure. I wanted her to see me — all of me.

When I was down to my boxers, Lil stood up and began peeling off her own clothes. Time slowed as each article of clothing fell to the floor. The tortoise had finally overtaken the hare. Nothing about me was rushing. I wanted this moment to last as long as humanly possible. I'd never seen anything more beautiful than she was in that moment. We groaned in unison as our skin was reunited. Our bodies hummed. We didn't need instructions. We knew what to do. Instinctively. Intrinsically. We knew.

After the most intense make-out session of my life, we both came up for air.

'Do you have—' Lil gasped.

I knew exactly what she meant, and I thanked my lucky stars, I did *have*. I rummaged through our clothes on the floor until I found my jeans. My fingers shook as I fumbled with the wrapper. I should've practised that part alone. But Lil came to my aid. She grabbed the wrapper, tore it open with her teeth and slid the condom on with ease.

She laughed. 'That was much easier than putting it on the sex ed banana.'

This is probably the appropriate time to fade to black. This isn't Fifty Shades of Fairview. But I will say this: it was perfect. That's not to say it wasn't without a few first-time hiccups. I was a bumbling fool to begin with, and I certainly lasted longer during our second time. But there was no pressure or judgement on either side. We figured it out as we went along. Together. And I wouldn't change a thing. Every kiss, every caress, every bite will be imprinted on my skin forever. I'll trace them with my fingertips for the rest of my days. I'm glad I waited. I'm glad my first time was with Lil. I felt like the luckiest guy alive.

CHAPTER NINETEEN

CAN'T TAKE MY EYES OFF OF YOU (I LOVE YOU BABY) — MS LAURYN HILL

Here's the thing about sex: it changes everything! People talk a lot about the deed itself. But no one prepares you for what happens after. I'm not talking about STDs or unplanned pregnancies, although there's no shortage of those horror stories, especially in small religious towns like Fairview. I'm talking about those weightless, not-a-care-in-the-world seconds when nothing else matters except you and the person beside you. That's the real revelation. I'd never felt more connected to another human in my entire life. How come you don't hear guys in the locker room talk about that? Orgasms are over in a blink. But that love-drunk bliss you're hit with afterwards lingers for days.

I don't know if anything will ever top my week at Lil's. Waking up next to her was like Christmas every morning. I might have been slow to lose my virginity, but that week it was well and truly exterminated. We lost count after day four.

Unfortunately, an invigorating state of bliss isn't the only byproduct of sex. Insecurity can also rear its ugly head. On our last day of parental freedom, my anxiety crept up on me like a stalker from a scary movie. The realisation that I was irreversibly in love felt like a knife to the heart. While she showered, I busied myself by making the bed. I frantically plumped the pillows and smoothed out every crease on the duvet with my hands. When I was done, I snooped around Lil's room in search of another distraction. *Timothy's Terrible Time Machine* was sitting on a shelf. I pulled it out and began flicking through the pages.

Lil emerged from the bathroom wrapped in a towel. Her damp hair dripped on the floor as she grabbed her blow-dryer and whipped her head back and forth in front of the mirror.

'WHAT DID YOU THINK OF THE BOOK?' I yelled over the roaring dryer.

'WHAT?'

I held up the book. 'DID YOU LIKE IT?'

Lil turned off the dryer. 'Oh yeah, it was . . . intense. I loved it.'

I could tell she was lying. Her eyes darted around the room like she was following an invisible mosquito.

'What was your favourite part?'

She marched to her wardrobe and started sifting through her colour-coordinated shirts. 'All of it,' she said. 'The whole thing. The pacing was great, and that ending . . . I mean, wow!'

'I cried so hard when Julie fell down the well,' I said.

'Oh my god, me too. Poor Julie!' she said, pulling a Ramones shirt over her head.

'You liar!' I laughed.

She froze like a cartoon bank robber. 'What do you mean?'

'There's no Julie!'

'Then who fell down the well?'

'No one! There's *no* well! You haven't even opened the book, have you?'

'Damn it, Brown! Don't go all *True Detective* on me! It's just a book.'

The whole thing was kind of funny. But in that moment I was hurt.

'I know it's just a book. But I wanted to share it with you. I love it when you share your art and music with me. It gives me a glimpse inside your weird and wacky brain. I just wanted to give you a peep into mine.

I thought you'd be interested.'

I could tell she felt terrible. I didn't mean to lay the guilt trip on so thick. But I was trying to be honest.

'I am interested,' she said, taking a seat next to me on the bed.

'You haven't even started it.'

'That's not true. I've tried. But I've been so busy.'

'But I gave it to you weeks ago! How long does it take to read one measly book?'

It came out harsher than intended. Lil leapt off the bed with a frustrated squeal.

'When you have severe dyslexia, too long, apparently.'

Yet again I felt like the world's biggest jerk.

'I'm sorry, I didn't know.'

Lil sat down again and squeezed my knee. 'No, I'm sorry. I should've told you.'

'If I wasn't such a huge ass, maybe you would've felt more comfortable.'

She grabbed my hand. 'Hey, don't do that. You're not a huge ass. You're a regular-sized ass. This isn't about you. I've always been insecure telling people about my dyslexia.'

'But you can tell me anything. You know that, right?'

'I'm starting to see that.' She smiled. 'Most people don't get it. Being dyslexic doesn't mean I'm less intelligent or anything. I just process things differently. I can read, but it takes me a little longer. And of course your favourite book had to be some thousand-page tome with a tiny font. I was intimidated. I tried finding an audio version, but it's also obscure AF. I was hoping you'd drop the subject until I got around to telling you.'

'Consider it dropped,' I said, kissing her on the nose. 'And thanks for telling me.'

'I sorta freaked when I realised you were such a bibliophile,' she said, 'because I knew I'd never share that with you. I have a complicated relationship with books. I don't hate them but I don't love them either.'

It suddenly dawned on me that I wasn't the only one who was afraid. Lil had her own set of insecurities to contend with.

'So, you're not into books. Big whoop! You're the smartest, most interesting person I know, and there are hundreds of other things we can share.'

'Hundreds?'

'Sure, there's video games, old horror movies, Jeff Goldblum, *Buffy the Vampire Slayer*, Oreo milkshakes, Dolly Parton, extra-crunchy peanut butter—'

'Okay, okay, I get it!'

'Wait, I have one more very important thing.'

'What?'

I leaned over and kissed her. 'So much cooler than reading.'

She agreed, but I still felt like a dick. I couldn't stop thinking back to all the times I'd badgered her about the damn book. Then a light bulb switched on. I couldn't erase the past, but I might be able to transform this debacle into the John Cusack boombox moment Lil deserved.

WE WERE PRETTY BLUE when our week of playing house came to an end. But at least I had a new master plan to focus on. As soon as I got home I grabbed my laptop and a USB stick, told Mom I was working on a summer assignment for extra credit and locked myself in my bedroom. It took me three whole days to complete. I barely had time to text Lil and I gave her the same spiel I'd given Mom about a summer assignment. After spending an entire week together, it was like going through withdrawal. But I needed to get this done before I saw her.

On day four Lil texted to ask if we could meet in the park. I slipped the USB into my pocket and skipped off. I couldn't wait to see her.

She was sitting on one of the swings, staring wistfully at the grass like it might be hiding the secrets to the universe. She looked upset.

'Hey stranger,' she said sullenly as I came up beside her.

'From lovers to strangers already? That's cold,' I quipped.

Her expression remained unchanged. She was clearly not in the mood for flippant humour.

'Is everything okay?' I asked, taking a seat on the swing next to hers.

'Peachy.'

'Really, 'cause I'm getting more of an unripe lemon vibe.'

She turned her head sharply and burned a hole in my face with her eyes. 'Look, if you're planning on dumping me, just do it! Don't avoid me like some spineless coward. You're better than that. At least I thought you were.'

This was not part of the script. I was about to perform my big romantic gesture, but I'd been thrown into the middle of a different play and I didn't know my lines.

'Avoid you . . . dump you . . . huh?' My mind scrambled to join the dots. 'Lil, I would never!'

'Then why'd you pull a Houdini? Right after we . . . Didn't it mean anything to you?'

I slapped my forehead. How could I have been so thoughtless?

'Lil, of course it did. It meant everything!'

'Then why do I feel like I've been ghosted?'

'Crap! This wasn't the plan. This is the opposite of the plan!'

My incoherence wasn't helping matters.

'Plan? Theo, this isn't a game. Maybe I should be the one dumping you!'

'I'm not playing games, I promise. Can we please stop talking about breaking up?'

'Then can you tell me what the hell is going on? You disappeared right after we'd slept together! What am I supposed to think?'

'I'm so sorry. I'm an idiot. I wanted to make up for the whole book thing. I felt terrible for pressuring you to read it. So, I wanted to do something special.'

I placed the USB on her lap. 'I made this for you. It's the reason I've been MIA the past few days.'

Lil stared at it blankly. 'Thanks. But what is it?'

'It's *Timothy's Terrible Time Machine*.'

'What do you mean?'

'It's the unofficial audiobook. Voiced by yours truly. Man, this went a lot smoother when I practised it in my head.'

'You made me an audiobook?' Her eyes were starting to water. I wasn't sure whether she was going to laugh or cry. 'How long is it?'

'Seventeen hours and 33 minutes. But it took longer to make. There were a lot of retakes in the beginning. But I think it turned out pretty good.'

A tear slid down her cheek. I was relieved she didn't laugh.

'You didn't have to do that,' she whispered.

'I know. I wanted to.'

She grinned wider than the Cheshire Cat from *Alice in Wonderland.*

'I hope you don't think it's stupid or cheesy.'

'Are you kidding? It's the most romantic thing anyone has ever done for me. You're a melting pot of fondue. Never change.'

'I should've called you. But I'm a terrible liar and didn't wanna blow the surprise. I didn't mean to freak you out.'

'You made me a frickin' audiobook! Who does that?' She laughed. 'All is forgiven.'

'I hope you like it.'

'I love it!'

'You haven't heard it yet.'

'I don't need to. I already love it. I've never felt like the kind of person worthy of big romantic gestures.'

'Are you serious? Everyone deserves at least one. But you deserve a million, Lil Sanchez, and I've only just begun.'

'I think I love you, Theodore Brown.'

'I think I love you, too.'

This was simultaneously the best and most terrifying moment of my life. As soon as the words left our mouths, I knew we were screwed. Because when I looked into Lil's eyes, I knew something she didn't. In 28 days, it would all be over.

CHAPTER TWENTY

TIME AFTER TIME — CYNDI LAUPER

You can't fight time
it's not some playground bully you push back
time does the pushing
and no matter how hard you try
there's no sneaking around it
no moving backwards
only forwards
unless you can travel faster than the speed of light?
didn't think so
there's no cheats or loopholes
we're all just slaves to the clock
marching on, one by one
tick-tock, tick-tock!

until we finally reach the ledge
and time nudges us forwards one very last
time
and suddenly, everything
stops
because it has won
just as it always has
and always will
time slowly strips everything away
condemning us to the dirt
still, we do all we can to delay the inevitable
we have our five a day
exercise
fucking moisturise
whatever it takes to feed our denial
but it always ends the same
time after time
resisting will only cause more pain
because in the end
time screws us all.

CHAPTER TWENTY-ONE

THIS TIME TOMORROW — BRANDI CARLILE

Exchanging the L-word with Lil sent me spiralling — hard. Hence the emo poem before. I kept telling myself I should be happy. But I couldn't stop thinking about how much it was gonna suck when I lost her. Sure, I knew this was coming. Believe me, I did. But I never anticipated our feelings would become this strong. I didn't think I'd fall in love and I sure as shit didn't think she'd love me back. I'd assumed I'd screw things up and she'd want nothing to do with me.

Turns out, I'm not total garbage at this whole boyfriend thing after all. Things couldn't be better between us. So I have no idea what's going to end us, only that it's going to happen.

It's like I'm experiencing PTSD. I'm not exaggerating. I keep getting flashbacks of my dad saying goodbye with those creepy zeros in his eyes, then I see his coffin being lowered into the dirt and I can't breathe. I try to calm myself by thinking about Ally. Maybe Lil will simply move out of this Podunk town too. The idea of never seeing her again still sucks, but it beats the thought of something bad happening to her. It's hard to avoid letting my mind go to those places. After all, Lil's family haven't shown any sign of moving. Her dad just got a huge promotion, and her mom is redecorating their bedroom. So it seems unlikely that this is an Ally-style sitch. I'd give anything for the tiniest clue about what is going to happen. I feel totally helpless.

I went to see Hey-Jude, and he gave me a copy of *The Power of Now*. I wanted to bash him over the head with it. Not gonna lie, I came close. I know he meant well, and I can see how the basic principles of the book could be helpful to someone in my predicament. But it's hard to live in *the now* when you're smacked with a literal countdown to the end of your relationship. I was doing my best to stay present and enjoy every moment we had left, but at some point I had to face the facts.

Summer is almost over. And goodbye summer means goodbye Lil!

I have no idea how I am gonna function without her. That probably sounds ridiculous. I mean, I did it before, I can do it again, right? But being alone was different before. I didn't know how amazing life could be. I can't just unknow that. I can't unknow her.

There is no one to blame but myself. I orchestrated this whole thing knowing it won't last. And now I am hopelessly devoted to a sinking ship. Lil and I have entered the third act of *Titanic*! No more sexy painting or steamy car rendezvous: we are headed straight for the iceberg and don't have a lifeboat. We don't even have a freakin' paddle or an ambiguously sized raft so people can argue over whether it was big enough to hold both of us.

We are screwed. Plain and simple.

I'd blame Lil too, but she can't help being so damn loveable. Hey-Jude also played a part in this. He's an enabler by his own definition. But the truth is, even if I could go back in time, I wouldn't do it any different.

Thankfully, Lil seems oblivious to my internal meltdown. She's too engrossed in *Timothy's Terrible Time Machine*. She calls me after every chapter to share her thoughts and predictions. She says she can tell which chapters I like best from the level of enthusiasm in my voice. Apparently, I get super-animated. So far she's pinpointed all my favourite parts with deadly accuracy, which means there must be something to her theory. She also suggested I consider making audiobooks for a living, which made me laugh.

Although, it was fun, and getting paid to read would rule. Lil's reserving her final verdict until she's finished the whole book.

THERE ARE MANY REASONS why this book means so much to me, and why I wanted to share it with Lil. It was written in the '90s by this Irish author named Keeva O'Donnell. *Timothy's Terrible Time Machine* is her only novel, and beyond this her life is as mysterious as the book. Some say this is because she used a pseudonym. Others believe she invented a time machine in real life and is travelling through time and space like Doctor Who. Hardcore fans have a theory that she altered the timeline so drastically, she wiped herself from existence. But I don't see how the book could still exist if this were true. There's a bunch of weird and complicated hypotheses online. I can't follow most of it. Time travel makes my head hurt.

But there's so much more to the book than time travel. It's about love, grief and the power of friendship. The story is told from the point of view of Timmy, this nerdy 16-year-old. After his best friend Benjamin is tragically killed in a car accident, Timmy invents a time machine to save him. Timmy feels partly responsible for Benji's death because the accident happened when he was on his way to meet him after they had this massive fight over their science project. But something goes horribly wrong every time Timmy travels back in time. It always ends the same. No matter what he does . . . Benji dies. To complicate matters, the time machine is a piece of shit. It's highly unstable and falling apart. Much like Timmy, it's more screwed up after each time-jump. By the end of the book, Timmy knows the time machine will only survive one more trip. It's his last shot to change the future. But he's so defeated by this point he doesn't even try. He realises he can't fight fate and gives up.

It's a grim lesson, I guess. But I've never related to a character more. To say it resonates would be a colossal understatement. I know Timmy is fictional, but I feel like he's the only person who truly gets me. Time is his biggest nemesis too.

BRB — my phone is buzzing!

Best book ever!

I JUST GOT OFF a video call with Lil. She finished the book! She said it's now her favourite too. She almost bounced right off her bed as she gushed over the ending.

Her analysis blew me away. She had a completely different interpretation. When I mentioned how devastating it was when Timmy gave up, she acted like I'd missed the mark or something.

'Okay, I know this book means a lot to you and you've read it a gazillion times,' she said cautiously, 'but I don't think Timmy gave up.'

'Really?'

'He learned he couldn't change the inevitable. Benji was going to die no matter what. So instead of wasting his last time-jump by running around desperately trying to save him, he uses it to have a blast with his bestie.'

My mind was blown! But Lil wasn't finished.

'He accepts that everything ends eventually. He realises that something isn't special because it lasts forever. It's more special because it doesn't. Everything is precious because nothing lasts. It's sort of beautiful in a melancholy kinda way.'

As soon as we got off the phone I reread the final chapter. Lil was right. It was beautiful. I'd been projecting myself onto the character so hard that I missed the point of the story.

I immediately sent Lil a message to thank her. I'd never read that book the same way again. It was like she rewrote the ending. Timmy's story wasn't so bleak anymore. And maybe mine wasn't either.

She helped me to accept that I couldn't control what was to come but I could control how I spent the time we had left. I decided to take Hey-Jude's advice after all and give Eckhart Tolle another shot. The next three weeks have got to be the best of our lives.

CHAPTER TWENTY-TWO

MY FAVOURITE GAME — THE CARDIGANS

Lil was about to turn 19, so over the next few days I planned a surprise road trip to celebrate. Lil's parents took some convincing, but after a little sweet talk and a glowing testimonial from Mom, we got the green light.

Mom is a legend! I honestly couldn't have pulled this off without her. Aside from reassuring Lil's parents that I wasn't going to kidnap their daughter and ruin her life, she let me borrow the car again. She even filled the tank. I reiterate, LEGEND!

Lil was buzzing when I picked her up. She had no idea where we were going, only that I had something special planned. And no, it wasn't the Botanical Gardens. Her parents were less enthused. Her dad looked like he didn't know whether to laugh, cry or punch me. Thankfully, I got off with a stern look that read, *Harm one hair on my daughter's head and your ass is grass, boy!* I simply nodded in agreement. It was the clearest non-verbal conversation I've ever had.

Watching Lil squeeze her gigantic leather duffel into the trunk was like a bad comedy skit. I got major déjà vu. It was just like when Ally showed up at my door bound for Alaska.

'So, where are we off to?' she asked, sliding into the passenger seat. Her eyes were wide with anticipation and too much caffeine.

'Judging by how much you've packed, I'd say New Zealand,' I laughed.

'It's hard to pack when you have no idea where you're going.'

'At least we can open up a small clothing boutique if we get stranded.'

'Spill it, Brown. I'm hopped up on coffee and not afraid to cut a bitch!'

'All in good time.'

'Seriously?'

'How 'bout a compromise? I'll give you the first clue.'

'*First!*' she shrieked. 'How many clues are there?'

'Chill. Only three.'

'*Three!* You are pure evil! You know I hate surprises.'

'Well, I have it on good authority you'll like this one.'

I reached into the glove compartment and pulled out the first clue.

'A doll?' Lil groaned. 'Wait, is that my old Barbie?' She grabbed it for closer inspection. 'It is her! How did you even get this? I threw Barberella Barquero away years ago.'

I grinned. I loved the fact that she named her Barbie.

'Well, your mom must've rescued Barberella from the trash.'

'My mother loaned you my Barbie . . . Now there's a sentence I never wanted to say.'

I handed Lil a gift to distract her from prematurely uncovering my painstakingly planned surprise.

'Is it another clue?'

'No, it's our road trip playlist. Every great adventure deserves an epic soundtrack.'

Lil beamed. 'You are too freakin' cute!'

As The Cardigans blasted through the speakers, our road trip had officially begun.

'I'm ready for the next clue,' Lil said after a couple of songs.

'Patience. We have a long journey ahead.'

'How long?'

'That would be another clue.'

She pulled her hair. 'I hate this game!'

'Really? I think it might be my new favourite.'

'Then when do I get the second clue?'

'At the halfway point.'

'How long will that take?'

'That would also be a clue.'

Lil threw herself back and folded her arms. But I could tell she was fighting a smile.

'I hate you!'

'Love you too.'

For the first time in my life I felt semi-adult. Here I was, taking my girlfriend on a romantic getaway that I'd planned and funded all by myself. If anyone had told me this at the start of summer, I would've said they were dreaming. But with the wind in our hair and the open highway stretching before us, it felt like anything was possible.

Stopping at a gas station for a restroom break about an hour into the drive, we had the bright idea of getting jumbo-sized slushies. It was a decision we would come to regret. Full bladders and long car rides are not friends. And naturally our bladders decided to scream bloody murder during a traffic jam on a busy highway. We had two options:

1. Wet ourselves and never speak of it. *What happens on the road stays on the road, right?*
2. We pull over and answer nature's call in

front of a packed-out audience. I mean, at least we didn't have to poop.

I suggested a third option involving the empty slushie cups. But Lil brought it to my attention that this would be much easier for me than it would be for her. 'If I'm peeing outside in front of a zillion people, you are too, Brown,' she growled.

'Don't worry, I've got your back. We're in this together, Thelma!'

'Don't make me laugh! This isn't the time for witty pop culture references,' Lil hissed, clenching her hands between her thighs, and bouncing up and down in her seat like she was on a pogo stick.

We had to move fast or events were about to get wet and wild in the worst way. I hit the brakes and we shot out of the car as if our lives depended on it.

'Damn it! I wish I'd worn a skirt,' Lil shrieked, pulling her jeans to the ground without warning. She shimmied her pants out of the line of fire with one hand and hiked her shirt down to hide her modesty with the other. 'Oh my god, yes!' she moaned in euphoria.

I quickly undid my zipper and let loose too. 'I don't care if the entire world is watching. This feels amazing!'

'Me neither. Nothing is ruining this moment for me.'

Is there a better sensation than relieving a full bladder that's come dangerously close to exploding? If there is, I haven't experienced it yet. And that's coming from someone who recently lost his virginity.

Our inhibitions returned once our bladders emptied. Lil shot to her feet. But she was back on the ground as quickly as she left it. She just collapsed without warning, and lay where she fell without moving a muscle. She was only out for a few seconds, but I was freaked. Was this the end of the trip already? I wondered whether we should turn back, or get her checked out at a hospital. But Lil was having none of it.

'I'm fine!' she insisted. 'I just stood up too fast and got a head rush. It's not a big deal.'

I still thought she should go for a check-up. But I trusted she knew her body better than I did, and she promised she'd talk to her doctor about it when she was home. Once we got back on the road, Lil was her sprightly self again.

'I think I've earned another clue after that ordeal, don't you?' she said.

'I told you, you'll get your next clue at the halfway point.'

'Where's that again?'

'Nice try!'

'Oh, come on! We just peed together! That kind of relationship milestone deserves commemoration.'

'Fine,' I relented. 'But then no more clues until our next stop.'

She rubbed her hands together in anticipation as I reached into my pocket. But her excitement quickly faded when I handed her the clue.

'A Jenga piece!' She sighed.

'Yes, but more importantly, what's it made from?'

Her eyes narrowed. 'Wood.'

'You got it! Now that's all you're getting,' I said.

She crinkled her nose and stared out the window in deep contemplation. 'My old Barbie and a wooden puzzle piece,' she mused, stroking her imaginary beard. 'Okay, we're either going to a strip club or a creepy vintage toy store.'

'I can promise you that I'll never take you to either of those places.'

'You may as well give me the final clue then. I'm never gonna figure this out.'

'You'll get the last clue in Lexington,' I let slip.

'Kentucky is the halfway point!' Her face lit up. 'Can we get spoon bread?'

Spoon bread is a Southern staple. It's basically corn pudding, made from corn muffin mix, canned cream corn, butter, milk and eggs. It's even better with cheese. It's creamy and delicious and you eat it with a spoon. Hence the name. We talked about food all the way to Lexington.

We were like rabid dogs by the time we arrived. We stumbled on a cute diner called Rustie's Ranch, lured in by the rich smell of butter and pastry. Lil practically screamed when she saw spoon bread on the menu. It tasted even better than it smelled. I ordered some fried chicken too. I mean, I couldn't stop in Kentucky and *not* try the fried chicken, and old Rustie's wiped the floor with Colonel Sanders. We waddled back to the car, content and full-bellied.

'Are you ready for your next clue?' I asked.

'Yes! Gimme!' Lil cupped her hands and held them out. 'This better not be more cryptic BS!'

'You can put your hands away. This clue isn't physical.'

'What does that mean?'

I hooked my iPod into the car and hit play on a second playlist I'd put together.

'Just listen.'

I turned up the volume, and Dolly Parton's '9 to 5' roared through the speakers.

'Don't toy with my emotions!'

'I would never!'

'Is Dolly a clue?' Lil's eyes darted back and forth as she put the puzzle pieces together. 'Barbie . . . Doll . . . Dolly . . . Wood . . . Are we going to—' She clasped her hand to her mouth, unable to finish her sentence.

'You got it!' I cheered. 'We're going to Dollywood!'

Lil proceeded to squeal the cutest squeal that has ever been squealed in the history of squeals.

'Theodore Brown! You are the best boyfriend in the entire universe!'

She kissed my face ferociously like a feral grandmother.

'Okay, *okay*!' I hollered, steadying the wheel. 'We still have to get there in one piece.'

We sang at the top of our lungs when the chorus hit. The trip was already worth every penny, and we hadn't even arrived at our destination. After some very questionable singing, Lil shared her childhood memories of Dollywood. Her parents had taken her when she was seven, and she'd always wanted to go back. She lit up when she talked about her favourite rides, the Chasing Rainbows Museum and the world-famous cinnamon buns from Aunt Granny's Restaurant. She had our entire weekend mapped out, including riding the Lightning Rod, a wooden rollercoaster that lives up to its name by travelling at 73 miles an hour. Lil said it's *a must*. I made a mental note not to eat beforehand.

WE LISTENED TO NOTHING but Dolly the rest of the way. *My Tennessee Mountain Home* played sweetly as we pulled into the smoky mountains. I slowed the car right down and tried to take it all in. I'd never seen anything so beautiful. We were surrounded by the most glorious trees and mountains, shrouded in a dreamlike fog that seemed to carry them into the sky. I'd seen similar images in paintings and photographs, but I'd chalked those up to romanticism and Photoshop. But this was real. This ancient utopia really exists.

'Don't forget to breathe.' Lil prodded me. 'It sure is something, ain't it?'

'It's everything Dolly said it would be,' I agreed.

Lil started unbuckling her seatbelt as soon as we reached Pigeon Forge, but I kept driving.

'I think you missed our stop for the park,' she said.

I had one last surprise up my sleeve. The cabin I'd booked was in Gatlinburg, just south of Pigeon Forge and bordering the Great Smoky Mountains National Park. The view was said to be spectacular.

Even so, I did a double take when we arrived and frantically checked my booking info to make sure we had the right place. I couldn't believe I was able to afford this. It looked like we were in the middle of some alpine Disney dreamscape, but with an unmistakable Tennessee flavour. It wouldn't have surprised me if little cartoon bluebirds fluttered overhead.

After we filled our lungs with the freshest air they'd ever breathed, we grabbed our bags and checked into our room. Another win. It had everything you could want in a traditional cabin: rustic wood and stone finishes, soft lighting, fluffy rugs and plaid sheets.

'Wow,' Lil said, slack jawed. 'Theo, this is perfect.'

Mission complete.

She dropped her bag on the floor and kissed me. Before I knew it, we were in our underwear on the bed. I was much more confident now. Lil harboured no insecurity or shame when it came to sex. She owned her sensuality in a way that invited you to do the same. She exuded nothing but pleasure. It was liberating and sexy as hell.

Afterwards, Lil fell asleep in my arms — and the darkness crept in like a thief in the night. I thought about how Lil had passed out earlier in the day. She said it was nothing. But what if it wasn't? What if this had something to do with her number? What if she was sick? It took all my willpower to brush those thoughts away.

I squeezed her tight and anchored myself in the present. In that moment, everything was perfect. We were happy and safe and in love.

CHAPTER TWENTY-THREE

I WILL ALWAYS LOVE YOU — DOLLY PARTON

Our first night in Tennessee was perfect. But at the crack of dawn we were torn from our dreamy cabin slumber when our phones shrieked in unison. Lil had decided one alarm wasn't enough; she wanted to be sure we left early enough to beat the queues for the Lightning Rod. My stomach churned at the thought. I couldn't think of a less relaxing way to start my day than by barfing on a rollercoaster. But Lil was the birthday girl and I wasn't gonna let my wimpy disposition spoil her fun.

We were out the door by seven and stopped at a nearby diner for a quick breakfast. I played it safe with tea and toast. Lil ordered coffee, fried tomatoes and vegan fritters. The smell was torture. When Lil had finished eating, I gave her one last surprise. Nothing big. The trip was her real gift. But I wanted her to have a memento to mark the occasion. So I'd made her a homemade birthday card. This was a ballsy move, considering Lil is a creative genius and I can barely draw stick people. But I played to my strengths and took the comedic route. I traced a picture of Dolly onto the card and added a speech bubble that read: *And I-EE-I-EE-I Will Always Love You.* Inside, I wrote: *Please Parton my lack of artistic talent and awful puns. Have a Dolly good Birthday. Love, Theo.*

It looked like something a child had made. But Lil loved it. 'No more. This is too much, Theo,' she gushed. 'How am I supposed to top all this when your birthday rolls round?'

Her words punched a hole through my chest. Because I knew she wouldn't have to worry about that. We'd be well past our expiration date by then.

'The card is corny,' I said. 'But I'm glad you like it.'

'Are you kidding? It's the best!' She leaned over the table and threw her arms around me.

We arrived at the park well over an hour before it opened. There was already a healthy queue forming. While we waited, we downloaded the Dollywood Park app with its maps, waiting times for rides and other helpful tips for getting the most out of our visit. Sergeant

Lil listed everything on our agenda like she was planning a covert mission.

'Remember, once we get inside the gates, we take a right and head straight for the Lightning Rod. Do not get distracted by the razzle dazzle. We'll have time to take everything in afterwards.'

'Yes, Ma'am!'

Lil blushed. 'Am I being super-extra right now?'

'Absolutely not. I love your enthusiasm. Besides, it's your birthday. You can be as extra as you like.'

'Then follow my lead, rookie. We're about to have the best day ever!'

DOLLYWOOD IS SOUTHERN CHARM personified. It's loud, colourful and unabashedly country. It somehow manages to feel both quaint and colossal. It's like small-town America and Disneyland had a baby, then wrapped her in a blanket of winding rollercoasters and magnificent smoky mountains. Lil grabbed my hand, and as soon as we were through the gates we sprinted straight to the Lightning Rod.

'Nice job, Brown!' she yelled, holding her hand in the air for a high-five. 'Can you believe it? We're the first ones here!'

'I can absolutely believe that,' I laughed, slapping her hand.

Being first in line was a blessing and a curse. On the plus side, it gave me less time to freak out. On the negative, it meant we'd be riding shotgun. Front and centre, with no one to hide behind.

Being catapulted at 73 mph and plummeting down a 165-foot drop is as terrifying as it sounds. It was a miracle I managed to keep my bland breakfast down. I felt like I was being pulled apart with every unexpected twist and turn. Frankly, I'll never understand why people pay actual money to terrorise themselves like that. I guess it's an acquired taste, like caviar. Personally, both make me want to hurl. But I lived to tell the tale, and at least I can say I've tried it.

'Come on!' Lil whooped as our car came to its juddering halt. 'Don't tell me that wasn't a rush.'

'Oh, it was a rush all right. An extremely fast, unnaturally high, terrifying rush.'

'But aren't you glad you did it?'

'I guess, in a I'm-glad-I'm-still-alive kinda way.'

'You're such a dork. Come on, let's get milkshakes at Red's.'

'We won't be going on that again, will we?' I asked.

'Nah, we've still got the Thunderhead, FireChaser, Blazing Fury and Tennessee Tornado to go.'

'Those all sound lovely. But let's get shakes afterwards. My regurgitated milkshake does not bring all the boys to the yard.'

'Eww!' Lil laughed. 'Hey, at least it might clear the lines.'

Once I'd survived all of Lil's aforementioned death contraptions, I was ready for the world's greatest milkshake. But not before one last scare. She had another dizzy spell on our way to Red's diner. It wasn't as bad as the one on the road, she didn't collapse completely, but it still sent shivers down my spine.

'Are you okay?' I gasped, grabbing her hand and holding her up as her legs seemed to give out beneath her.

'I'm fine. Just dizzy from the rides.'

Had this been an isolated incident I probably would have believed her. But my brain loves any excuse to play worst-case scenario.

'Don't look so worried, Silly,' Lil said softly. 'I just need to eat something. That's all.'

I did my best to brush it off. But I checked the Dollywood app when Lil wasn't looking and made a mental note of the location of the nearest first-aid station.

Red's Drive-In is straight out of the 1950s, minus the casual sexism, homophobia and racism. It even has one of those retro jukeboxes you see in the movies. I desperately wanted a burger and fries, but Lil insisted we save our appetites for Aunt Granny's Restaurant. After one sip of my towering salted caramel milkshake, I forgot burgers existed. Lil wasn't exaggerating. They really were the best. But my anxiety returned once the sugar high wore off.

'Are you okay?' Lil asked, clearly picking up on my change of mood.

'Yeah, this place is amazing!'

'Then why do you look like someone spiked your milkshake with vinegar?'

There was no hiding it. I was struggling. I wanted everything to be perfect, but the more perfect things were, the more it hurt.

'I don't wanna lose you,' I said.

Lil nodded. 'I get it.'

'You do?'

'You're experiencing foreboding joy.'

'Huh?'

'It's Brené Brown 101. You're freaking out because things are great. When life runs too smoothly, we prepare for a crash landing.'

'I guess that makes sense.'

'Brené don't guess, she knows. Trust and relax.'

'But what if preparing for a crash landing is necessary? What if you know something bad is coming?'

'Theo, you can't know that. No one can. This is a friggin' awesome day! Give yourself permission to enjoy it. The world will keep spinning. I promise.'

'You sound like Hey-Jude.' This sounded more contemptuous than I'd intended.

'And that's bad?'

'You don't understand. It's not that simple for me.'

'Why?' she shot back.

'I just know things,' I said. I had no intention of saying more. This wasn't the time or place to open Pandora's Box. But my motor mouth kept running. 'Like when I lost my dad, or when Ally moved away. I knew. Before it happened.'

'Are you saying you're psychic or something?'

'I wish. If I was psychic I could do something to fix things, and I wouldn't be so useless.'

'Don't say that! You're not useless. You're amazing. Just look what you've done for me.'

My eyes began to water. 'I'm sorry, I'm babbling. I think the rides made me lightheaded too. Please, forget I said anything. It's your birthday. Let's have fun.'

Lil placed her hand on my shoulder and looked deep into my eyes. I think Wordsworth might be right about the eyes being windows to the soul, because at that moment I felt totally naked. 'Theo, it's me,' she said. 'You can tell me anything.'

'I know. And I will. Just not here. Not now.'

I wanted nothing more than to break down and tell her everything. But I wasn't about to ruin her day. Besides, it wouldn't do any good. Why should we both suffer? Telling her would be selfish.

She brushed my hair out of my eyes and kissed my

cheek. 'Whenever you're ready to talk, I'm here.'

'We can talk about it when we get home. Just promise you won't think I'm crazy.'

'You're far from crazy. You're the sweetest guy I've ever met.'

AFTER RED'S, WE BOARDED the Dollywood Express for a five-mile train ride around the park. This probably makes me a grandpa, but this was my kind of ride. We held hands and soaked up the scenery in silence. Lil laid her head on my shoulder, and I wished the train ride would never end.

But our stomachs had other plans. They growled in unison. A milkshake wasn't gonna cut it much longer. Next stop just had to be the famous Aunt Granny's. It's exactly how it sounds — like your sweetest aunt and granny went into business. The food is mighty, an all-you-can-eat buffet of Southern staples: fried chicken, pot roast, catfish with lemon tartar sauce, corn puddin', mashed potatoes and gravy, mac n cheese, honey-glazed root vegetables, the list goes on . . . We ate until it hurt.

'We're done with rollercoasters, right?' I groaned.

'For sure. Even I'd barf at this point.'

'I'm sorry for being a buzzkill earlier.'

'Don't apologise for your feelings. This is the best birthday I've ever had.'

'I'm glad. But why Dolly?' I asked. 'The only other time I've seen you light up like this is when you talk about your art.'

'I guess she's always been there. Her music's been in my life since I was a baby. The first time we came to Dollywood, my parents argued the whole way here. But as soon as those gates opened, everyone was smiling. Dolly's the one thing we could always agree on. That vacation is probably the most fun we've ever had together as a family.'

'I can't imagine your parents arguing. They seem so perfect.'

'And there's your red flag. Perfect is always a lie. Underneath the shiny veneer, we've become strangers. Sure, we eat dinner together and sleep under the same roof, but I don't think we know each other anymore.'

'Sounds lonely.'

'Don't get me wrong, I love my parents. I'm grateful for everything they've done for me. But I've never felt good enough for them. I'm not girlie enough for my mom. Fuck gender stereotypes! Still, she keeps buying me makeup and dresses, even though I'm more likely to *date* the kinda girl who's into that stuff. Trouble is, I'm not into business or sport like my dad either.' She sighed. 'They don't get my art. They say they do, but it's bullshit. They see it as a cute hobby, not a valid career prospect. I know it sounds pretentious, but if I'm not making art, I don't feel like me. I wish just once they'd see me instead of the person they want me to be.'

'You should tell them,' I said. 'Word for word. Exactly like you just told me.'

'I've tried. They say they just want me to have a back-up plan. Which is smart, I get it. Making a career in the arts is hard. But they put way more emphasis on this *supposed* back-up. Deep down, I know they don't believe in me. And that sucks! Because I know I've got what it takes.'

'I believe in you. Fancy art college or not. Your work speaks for itself.'

'Thanks. I believe in you too. So don't forget about me when you're a bestselling author.'

'As long as you don't forget about me when you're a famous artist.'

'Deal.' She beamed.

My heart ached. I had no idea Lil felt so alienated at home. Growing up, I was so jealous of kids on her block with their big houses and nuclear families. I guess the old cliché is true: you never know what's going on behind closed doors. I felt a sudden burst of gratitude. Mom and I don't have much, but our house is filled with love, and that's what counts. I know Dolly would agree with me on that.

Now that we'd both unloaded, it was time to get back to fun. We let our dinner digest as we visited the

Chasing Rainbows Museum. Lil was in heaven. The tour kicks off with a welcome from Dolly herself! Sort of. The real Dolly is obviously too busy making music. But you're greeted by a hologram of the Queen of Country and it's pure magic. After her warm welcome, she turns into a butterfly and flutters away, leaving you free to explore her treasure trove of wonders, including a replica of the famous handstitched coat of many colours. Each item plays a part in telling Dolly's iconic *rags to rhinestones* story.

There was just one more stop before we headed back to the cabin. It was the last thing on Lil's bucket list. Dollywood's DreamMore Resort has an actual treasure chest. Enclosed in a glass case behind a velvet rope sits a wooden box that contains Dolly's final song. Nobody will hear it until January 19 2046, when the box is opened for Dolly's hundredth birthday. Only Dolly has the foresight to map out her career for an entire century. Genius!

We ended what can only be described as the best day of my life under the stars in our cabin's very own private hot tub. Well, that was nearly the end. Needless to say, things got even steamier once we left the tub.

CHAPTER TWENTY-FOUR

PETRIFIED — OMAR APOLLO

Four days ago, I was having the time of my life in Tennessee with my girlfriend. Now I'm frantically pacing back and forth in my room like a glitching Sims avatar. Alone. I've barely spoken to Lil since we got home. She's ignoring my calls. Everything was fine when I dropped her off. We laughed the entire drive home. I have no idea what's going on. We really need to stop ghosting each other like this.

Thankfully, the countdown stops when we're apart. So, we'll still have 19 days left when I see her again. But the separation anxiety is killing me. If staying away from Lil would keep her safe, I'd willingly never see her again.

But as I learned during my final days with Ally, nothing I do matters. The number is predestined. Meaning I'm powerless, as usual. I just wish we could have stayed in that cabin forever. But two nights was all my broke ass could afford. I haven't had a good night's sleep since I got back and the nightmares have returned. The night I dropped Lil home was the worst . . .

I'm strolling through the park. It's late. I can hear Lil calling my name. She sounds distressed, like she's in danger. I follow her mournful cries until I find her on the swing set. I approach cautiously from behind. There's something unnatural about her movements. She lurches back and forth stiffly. It's as though the swing is moving of its own accord, rocking her involuntarily. I notice she's only holding one of the ropes. She's pointing at something ahead with her free hand. I move closer to see what she's staring at. I freeze. Lil's pointing at a tombstone. Lily Sanchez *is carved into the polished grey stone. There's an open grave below. I gently tap Lil's shoulder. I want to carry her away. But her neck jerks with an awful crack, before spinning 180 degrees. Her eyes are as black as the night sky. They glisten like marbles. A ghostly white zero haunts the centre of each. 'DON'T TOUCH ME!' Lil shrieks. 'EVERYTHING YOU TOUCH DIES!' I fall to the ground. Lil is violently ripped from the swing set by an invisible force. She claws at the dirt as she's dragged into the open grave. She lets out the most terrifying screech as the dirt falls on top of her. I try to get up, to run to her, to save her. But I'm paralysed. Dirt rains on her until the grave is full. And she's gone. Buried alive.*

I woke up drenched in sweat, screaming Lil's name. I texted her straight away to make sure she'd booked an appointment with her doctor. She told me she went as soon as we got home and had some blood tests done; she'd let me know the results. But I haven't heard from her since. I've tried calling several times, but it goes straight to voicemail. That whole *absence makes the heart grow fonder* spiel is horse shit. Absence makes the heart malfunction is a more accurate sentiment. I guess that's a little too real for a Hallmark greeting card.

I'm trying not to jump to conclusions, but something must have shown up on those tests. What other explanation is there? How else could I go from the world's best boyfriend to vanishing from her plane of existence? It makes zero sense, unless she needs space to process bad news . . .

I don't want to be clingy, but if I don't hear from her by tomorrow, I may cave. I want to hold her in my arms and tell her everything will be okay. I keep telling myself she'll call when she's ready — when she needs me. But I'm running out of distractions and I've bitten my fingernails down to the nubs.

I talked to Hey-Jude about it. He said I'm doing the right thing by giving Lil space. He believes there's a perfectly reasonable, non-fatal explanation. But that's

Hey-Jude for you. Forever the optimist.

And maybe he's right in this instance . . . My pocket is vibrating. Finally, a text from Lil.

Sorry. I didn't mean to ghost.

Things have been loco!

Is everything OK?

Can we talk in person?

When?

Nowish?

Where?

Park. I'm already here.

On my way.

Thnx. I'm on the swings.

CHAPTER TWENTY-FIVE

COULD CRY JUST THINKIN ABOUT YOU — TROYE SIVAN

I guess everyone's had one of those moments when time slows and everything gets muffled before grounding to an earth-shattering halt? Sometimes you see these tidal waves coming a mile off, but they still knock the wind out of your lungs when they hit. Their impact draws an irrefutable line in the sand, and nothing is ever the same.

That was yesterday. That was Lil Sanchez.

I met Lil in the park by the swings as promised. The same swing set from my nightmare — the one where we said 'I love you' for the first time. It's funny, in a cruel sort of way, how endings and beginnings often intertwine like some karmic joke.

The park was empty aside from Lil, who was swinging wistfully. It was dusk and the sky was a glorious shade of fuchsia. The scene might have been romantic under different circumstances.

Lil feigned a smile. But it was the sort of smile you get at a funeral, or when you fail your driver's test. It held that delightful blend of sorrow and pity that says, *Hang in there, bud.*

'Hey,' Lil said, tugging on her sweater sleeve. 'Sorry for pulling a Geri Halliwell. I didn't mean to break up the band.' She stared at the ground as she spoke. 'Something came up. Something huge. And I needed time to think.'

I swallowed the lump in my throat. I'd been holding it for days, so it felt good to finally choke it down. 'You don't need to apologise. Whatever it is, I'm here.'

Lil nodded to the swing next to her. 'You might wanna sit down.'

I took a deep breath. 'It doesn't matter what the test results say,' I assured her. 'We'll get through it. Together.'

'Test results?' Lil covered her mouth in horror. 'Oh crap! I'm so sorry!'

'Stop apologising. You've done nothing wrong.'

'Yes, I have! I'm an asshole, I forgot all about the stupid tests! You must've been worried sick.'

'I was — I am . . . Wait, what's going on?'

'The test results were fine.'

I shook my head. 'But what about your dizzy spells and the fainting?'

'I was low on iron and B12. They gave me a few supplements. I'm fine.'

'You are?' I threw my head back and thanked the heavens.

'Being veggie, I'm usually more mindful of my diet. But I've been pulling all-nighters and missing meals to finish my portfolio on time.'

'Portfolio?' I felt like I'd missed a pivotal episode of a beloved TV series.

'Remember that really great art school I told you about?'

It took me a minute, but I remembered. It was at the start of summer — the first time I visited her house. 'Yeah?'

'I got in!'

I scratched my head, trying to catch myself up to speed. 'But I thought you missed the submission date?'

'I did. But you convinced me to give it a shot anyway.'

'I did?'

'You said my art was so good they'd make an exception.'

'I did.' I repeated, this time recalling the conversation more clearly.

'I guess the compliment went to my head. I applied

after you left that evening. I didn't think I had a shot in hell.' Her eyes widened as she leaned forwards on the swing. 'They got in touch a few weeks ago. They said they were impressed with my work. I assumed they were gonna suggest I apply again next year . . . but it turns out a spot has become available.'

'That's amazing!' I beamed.

'They wanted to see more of my work before they made a final decision. So, they gave me a special assignment to prove I could handle the course. I've been working like a maniac ever since. Hence the lack of sleep, skipped meals and subsequent wooziness.'

'But you did it! You got in! I knew you could do it!' I jumped off my swing and threw my arms around her. She fell forwards onto my chest, I lost my footing and the two of us landed in a heap on the grass.

'I would've told you,' she said. 'But I didn't wanna jinx it.'

She still seemed subdued, but as we lay on the grass watching the sunset, my anxiety melted. I'd been preparing for bad news — worst-case scenario type news. This was like hitting the jackpot instead. But when I looked into Lil's eyes, I saw we weren't out of the woods yet. Her number was still a dwindling 19.

'Are your parents cool with it?' I asked.

'They were sceptical at first. But they came around when the Dean rang and explained what an amazing opportunity this is. I'm sure they're still worried I'm throwing my future away. But they said it's my decision, and that's a better response than I'd hoped for.'

'Then why aren't you screaming or doing backflips?'

'I was — for about 10 seconds. Then reality hit. It's a lot to take in.'

'But this is your dream.'

'Yeah, but I've never been that far from home.'

'Where's the school?' I couldn't remember if she'd told me. The start of summer felt like a lifetime ago.

She looked away before answering. 'London.'

'London, Ontario?' I asked hopefully.

'London, England.'

'As in tea and crumpets, Buckingham Palace, halfway-around-the-globe London?'

'That's the one.'

'Jolly good!' That is when the tidal wave hit.

Lil laid her head on my chest. 'Yup, right there with ya.'

We lay quietly for a long time, staring at the sky as it changed colour and the first stars appeared.

'This is good news,' I said, breaking the long silence.

I meant it. All things considered, this was the best news possible. It sure as hell beat the nightmares I'd been cooking.

'Then why do you look so sad?'

'Same reason as you, I guess. But I couldn't be

happier for you. Honestly. You earned this and you should be excited.'

'I am. I'm ecstatic. But it still sucks!'

'It does. But it also kinda doesn't.'

'What about us? We have something special here.' She'd never sounded so vulnerable.

I stroked her hair. 'We do.'

'We can't give that up like it means nothing!'

'A wise woman once told me something isn't special because it lasts forever.'

'Everything is precious because nothing lasts,' Lil finished.

I kissed the top of her head. 'Like I said, you're the smartest person I know.'

I felt her shiver. The moon had brought a chill along with it. 'So where do we go from here?' she said.

'I'm not sure. I guess we start by making the most of every second we've got left.'

'Careful, you're starting to sound like your therapist.'

I laughed. 'Yeah, I guess I am.'

EPILOGUE

I CAN SEE CLEARLY NOW — JOHNNY NASH

I wanted to be 100 percent present during my final weeks with Lil. I'd finally got the hang of that *Power of Now* stuff Hey-Jude was always harping on about. But the truth is our last days together were the definition of bittersweet. On the surface, there was nothing remarkable about them. We watched movies, played video games, listened to music and talked endlessly. Normal everyday stuff — yet they were the best days of my life.

The night before she left, Lil asked if we should try the long-distance thing. I'm certain she only suggested it out of courtesy. She's a realist. I told her I'd rather she remembered me as the world's best boyfriend instead of some ball-and-chain. She was off to art college — she should be out partying and hooking up with tattooed women with shaved heads and lip piercings. She laughed before admitting my idea sounded hot.

She managed to persuade her parents to let me drive her to the airport after she'd said goodbye to them at home. It felt right, ending on one last road trip together. Of course, I expected to see two zeros in her eyes that day. But as we kissed each other goodbye at the departure gate, the number 1 sparkled like a parting gift.

Knowing I'd see her again was like placing a Band-Aid over my heart. It didn't stop the bleeding, but it slowed it down enough to survive the goodbye. I won't lie, it took weeks to dress the wound properly, and even longer for it to heal over. The mark Lil left on me will never fade completely — and I don't want it to. The scar reminds me that a love like ours is possible. I used to think losing her would leave me with nothing but despair. But I couldn't have been more wrong. She gave me the opposite of despair. Lil gave me hope.

I HAVE NO IDEA when our last day together will be. Could be soon. Could be years from now. Time will tell. I'm not sad about it anymore. It's nice knowing we still have one last song to sing. I've learned that some people are only meant to be a part of our lives for a season or two. That doesn't mean they don't matter or they don't care. It's just how life is sometimes. I'll never forget my summer with Lil. Losing her was torture. But knowing her was everything. If I had a time machine, I wouldn't change a thing. I'd do it all over again.

No matter how much time passes, I know I'll think of Lil now and then. I'd like to think she'll think of me too. Maybe when a Dolly song comes on the radio, or she stumbles on an old horror movie while surfing the channels. And I hope it makes her smile. Our time together was fleeting. But for one sparkling moment, we meant the world to each other. And that moment can never be erased. It'll always be there. Etched on our timelines like a beautiful scar.

We still talk on the phone. She's clearly having a blast. She's with her people now and her work is on fire, exploding like a paint-filled volcano. Her art isn't the only thing that's heating up. She said the women on campus are insanely hot too. I'm certain the next person she dates won't have a penis.

Things with her folks have also improved. She said she's never felt closer to them, which is ironic considering she's never been further away. Apparently, they couldn't be more supportive. They're even talking about moving to London. So that explains her number. I'd been trying to figure out why she wouldn't come to see me when she visited them for the holidays. But I'm glad she knows they believe in her.

As for me — I'm back at college. In fact, I just scored an A+ for my latest short story. My professor said I must have had an eventful summer. Apparently, my writing has a pulse now. Whatever that means. He also said my characters are more three-dimensional. I guess that makes sense. It's much easier to write about people when you're not shutting them out.

And that's not all that's changed. I've stopped seeing Hey-Jude, at least in a therapist capacity. We both agreed that I'm ready to fly solo for a while. I've come a long way, and I know where he is if I need to book an impromptu session. I assumed I'd be in therapy with him for the rest of my life, thanks to the gigantic number I'd seen in his eyes when we first met. Turns out there may be another explanation. Involving my mother!

Mom has a new guy. His name is Joshua — and he's Hey-Jude's brother. His dress sense isn't quite as sharp, but he's pretty fly for a straight dude. He owns his own record store and produces music on the side. I haven't seen Mom this happy in a long time. It's awesome. And judging by Joshua's number, he's here to stay. Wouldn't it be crazy if Hey-Jude ended up being like my uncle?

And there is one more thing. It's not a big deal. I'm not even sure what it means yet. But I bumped into this guy at Joshua's record store the other day. His name's Andre and he works there on weekends. I bought a Troye Sivan record and we got talking at the checkout. It was pretty brief, and the whole thing was awkward as hell, to be honest. But he was sweet and had a kind smile, and . . . his number took me by surprise. I don't know what the future holds, but according to his eyes, this guy's gonna be a big part of mine.

I get it now. Time isn't my enemy. It's a gift. My relationship with Lil helped me to accept my condition. I don't see it as a curse anymore, and I'm not gonna spend my days fighting it. From now on I'm not even going to avoid looking at people's numbers. I'm going to embrace my gift and use it to ensure I never take another second for granted. Because time, and the people we spend it with, are more valuable than anything in the world. As the smartest person I've ever known once said:

'Something isn't special because it lasts forever. It's more special because it doesn't. *Everything* is precious because *nothing* lasts.' — Lil Sanchez

ACKNOWLEDGEMENTS

I doubt many people besides my parents will read this part, so that's probably the best place to start: Look Mum and Dad, I wrote a book!

Seriously though, there are so many people to credit for making this dream come true. It really does take a village, and I offer my sincerest gratitude to the following . . .

Carol and Eamon Devenney, these pages wouldn't exist without both of you, and the delulu levels of self-esteem you instilled in me from a young age. I wish every queer kid was blessed with parents like you.

Keeva O'Donnell, for reading everything I've ever written, most of which will thankfully never see the light of day. Your honesty is invaluable. Cheers bestie. Sidenote: You may recognise this name from the book. Who else would I name Theo's favourite author after?

Jo McColl, my fairy godmother in cowboy boots!

You are an incredible boss, businesswoman and friend. I am indebted to you and my teammates at Unity Books for your endless support. You also introduced me to the next person on this list. So, to say you've been instrumental to this process is no exaggeration.

Jenny Hellen, and the amazing crew at Allen & Unwin. Thank you for believing in my story and exceeding my expectations during every step of the way. You are all stars.

Jane Parkin, I couldn't have asked for a better editor. You are simply the best. My experience with you has sharpened my craft.

Alissa Dinallo, for the stunning cover. My biggest fear was that I wouldn't like the cover of my own book. But I loved every design you came up with. It's a shame we couldn't release them all as variants like a Taylor Swift record.

Sophie Watson, for illustrating Theo's beloved leather jacket. It's just right.

Pablo A. Correa, for the superb author photos. You managed to mask my awkwardness and make me look somewhat cool. You're a true magician!

Claire Mabey and Hera Lindsay Bird, for helping me navigate this incredible industry I've snuck into. Your generous tips and advice won't be forgotten.

My sisters, Donna and Emma, for being beautiful badass humans. You are both a constant source of inspiration to me and my writing. And my brothers, Aaron and Cal, you're okay too.

Ronald Andres Molina Lozano, for holding my hand on the way to that first publishing meeting, and for jumping up and down with me in the middle of the street when we got the good news. Celebrating with you made this infinitely more special. Gracias, mi amor. Te amo.

Bookshops and booksellers everywhere, you are lighthouses of hope, guiding our wandering imaginations safely to new worlds. You provide needed escapism before returning us to the world we inhabit with a better understanding of it. You are vital. Now more than ever.

Shout-out to Whitcoulls for giving me my very first job as a bookseller, and to the lovely Joan McKenzie for encouraging my early writing.

And finally, the readers. If you're holding this book and aren't one of the aforementioned; thank you for choosing my book over the endless treasure troves lining the shelves. I'm both humbled and grateful beyond measure. Stories don't come alive until somebody reads them, and you breathed life into mine. I hope you fell in love with these characters as I did. They became so real to me that, at times, it felt like they were writing themselves and I was just along for the ride. And man, what a ride we had! It was hard saying goodbye to Theo and Lil. Not gonna lie, tears were shed. I imagine this is what it feels like when your kids leave home. They're just out there doing their own thing now, and I hope the world will be kind. I miss them. But I'm also very proud of them.

Plus, the best thing about stories is that there's always another waiting to be told . . .

For those who may be struggling or are worried about others in their life, there are always people you can turn to for support. Here are a few of them:

New Zealand

www.1737.org.nz
www.headstrong.org.nz
www.lifeline.org.nz
www.youthline.co.nz

Australia

www.headspace.org.au
www.kidshelpline.com.au
www.lifeline.org.au
www.reachout.com.au

DANIEL DEVENNEY was born in Donegal, Ireland. He has been a passionate bookseller in Aotearoa New Zealand for over a decade and currently works at Unity Books. He lives in Auckland with his fiancé, Ronald. When he's not reading or writing, he's probably listening to Dolly Parton or rewatching *Buffy the Vampire Slayer*. *Counting Down with Theodore Brown* is his debut novel.